INFINITE DARK

VOLKRANIAN CHRONICLES: II

PAGE MORGAN

CHAPTER ONE

I CAN'T BELIEVE we invited the aliens to our high school.

I knew it was a terrible idea the moment our principal announced the planned visit. Now, here I am, on the football field bleachers, hunching my back, and trying to use Hannah Garrett as a shield. It's pointless; she's five-foot-two and thin as a potato stick. I zip my jacket all the way to my throat and flip up the hood, but it doesn't matter.

The Volkranian can see me. His stare prickles my skin.

It's all Miss Chapman's fault. She's the one who suggested Alton High should bring in a Volkranian for Culture Week to talk about their people, their customs, and their general *alienness*. Our art teacher has been a Peaceful Settlement supporter ever since the invaders stopped attacking and killing us seven months ago.

It isn't that I'm not for Peaceful Settlement, too. I have the freaking pin on my book bag and the decal on my locker door, just like everybody else. But this morning, I nearly faked being sick so I could stay home.

I tug my hood down over my forehead until my eyes are

practically covered. Beside me, Sam Streeter nudges my leg. "Pen? Why do you have your jacket on?"

"I'm cold."

"It's seventy degrees."

Sure, it's a sauna inside my rain jacket, but a little sweat is well worth protecting my secret. No one here knows what happened to me last October during the two days a Volkranian cityship hovered over New York City, and I'd like to keep it that way.

If the visiting diplomat recognizes me, and if people notice, the truth might come out—that I'd been aboard the first cityship. That I'd already met Volkranians. Talked to them. Argued with them. Nearly been killed by a number of them.

And I'm pretty sure I'd fallen in love with one of them, too.

But I don't want to think about Rowan right now.

"I must be coming down with something," I say to Sam and pull the hood forward some more.

A person higher up on the bleachers shushes us. Sam bumps my shoulder as he twists and raises his hand, most likely giving the person the finger.

In the football field, there's a stage rigged with a microphone and sound system, brown metal folding chairs, and a Peaceful Settlement banner trimming the stage floor. Next to the stage, the high school band finishes up a wheezing rendition of "God Bless America." The drummer is painfully offbeat, and there's a trombone that sounds like it's going through puberty. A few extra cymbal crashes make me grit my teeth before all goes quiet.

"I think my ears are bleeding," Sam mutters.

I kick his ankle while Principal Richards clears her throat and taps the microphone.

"Well, that was a...*lovely* effort from the Alton High student band!" There's a smattering of half-hearted applause. "And now, we are honored to have the Fleet Commandant of Volkron Six joining us today! We at Alton High are dedicated to promoting Peaceful Settlement and want you to know you'll find a warm welcome here."

More applause, but even though three other area high schools have also come to see the Volkranian diplomat, the clapping is cautious and weak. A dozen news vans have set up along the sidelines, most of them major stations, though there are a few grassroots reporters from Internet-only channels that track the Volkranians on a twenty-four-hour basis.

I peek out from under my hood as the clapping falls off—and immediately regret it.

A pair of silvery eyes connect with mine. It's like an ice cube dropping down the back of my shirt. The warden's stony expression is the same one I remember well, and I'm sure he couldn't care less about finding a warm welcome here at Alton High.

The warden scowls at me another second before turning it loose on the rest of the crowd. Only now, he doesn't hold the ranking of warden, does he? He's fleet commandant—a position that belonged to Rowan for all of a few hours, before he and the original Volkron Six ship were sent back into outer space by the Sovereign.

The first Volkron Six had looked like a mountainous city with upside down skyscrapers, its ridges made of black metal and reflective glass. Thousands of Volkranians had been aboard when the Sovereign, over Tokyo, took remote command of the cityship and sent it hurtling out of Earth's atmosphere as punishment for the deadly attacks on New York City—something the first fleet commandant of Volkron Six, Rowan's father, had ordered without permission from the Sovereign.

Now, the warden commands a pale pink, egg-shaped spacecraft above New York City. Considering it looks like a giant Easter egg, the new Volkron Six isn't nearly as intimidating. Its smooth surface changes color at sunset, turning a fluorescent orange, and that's also when you can see the strips of windows that wrap around the ship, one on top of another like thousands of giant elastic bands. And at night, instead of the violet light the first cityship had cast, this one casts a silvery glow, like the warden's irises.

"Thank you for extending the invitation," he replies to Principal Richards. His rough voice blasts through the microphone, and I jump.

Something is wrong. He shouldn't be at Alton High. He's the fleet commandant. He's important. *President-of-the-United-States* important. Why would he accept an invitation from us?

"You should probably uncover your head," Sam whispers. "He keeps looking up here. What if you're offending him with that hood?"

"I'm not offending him."

"How do you know that? Richards hasn't even asked him questions about his culture yet. It could be a cultural faux pas."

"Like you care about offending the Volkranians," I say.

Sam is a Salvager, one of the "Take Back the World" types that have been gaining momentum the last few months. Like the rest of the Salvagers, Sam despises the Volkranians. And considering my mom and I are currently living with him and his little sister, it's probably best if he doesn't find out about Rowan.

I didn't know Sam before the attacks. He's the kid my mom helped survive the Lincoln Tunnel riots during the invasion. The day after my mom and I were reunited—the third day of the invasion, and the day electricity and communications were restored to the world—we'd sifted through our home's wreckage trying to gather up what we could. There wasn't much. Some clothes, a fire-safe box filled with documents and some emergency cash, and thankfully, our cat Mister Mister.

But my mom bawled when she found the photo albums of

my little brother, Ollie, burnt to nearly unrecognizable crisps. I'd cried too, but I'd wiped my cheeks and told her that it wasn't all we had left of him. There were still thousands of pictures of Ollie online in her cloud, and when we got a computer, we'd access them and print them out again. It had been enough to calm her down, to draw her away from the edge of one of her panic attacks. And when I suggested we go check on the two kids she'd helped in the Lincoln Tunnel, my mom had quickly focused.

She led the way to a side street off the interstate, to the garage of the teenage boy she'd been caring for during the two days I'd been with Rowan. Sam's leg was healing okay, but his little sister, Hayden, had developed a wracking cough and a fever. Sam hadn't known what to do. Their dad had been delivering tires in Brooklyn, and their mom had been working in a hotel. They never made it back from the city.

Being a nurse, my mom easily fell into the role of caregiver for Sam's sister. We stayed with them for a few days, until Hayden's fever broke, and she looked to be on the mend. Sam told us we were welcome to stay for another few days if we wanted. And when Hayden started asking me to read her a bedtime story and giggling when my mom tickled her behind the ears while braiding her long, dark hair, Sam asked us to stay with them indefinitely.

So that's where we've been for the last seven months. It's a small, two-bedroom apartment above a sprawling garage, but it's better than being homeless. And unlike a lot of people fleeing the city for other towns and cities that don't have spacecrafts hovering overhead, my mom and I can't leave. This is where my dad knows where to find us.

If he ever comes home.

"Seriously, Pen. Take the freaking hood down."

Have I mentioned yet that Sam's a pain in the ass?

"*Fine.*" The warden knows I'm here anyway. I push back the hood and take a hesitant glance toward the stage.

The warden's gaze fastens onto me. I hold his glare, though my cheeks are warm.

Principal Richards reads a question from the stack of index cards the students submitted over the last week. "What kinds of music do the Volkranians listen to?"

Some guy raises a hand and shouts, "That was my question!"

A burst of laughter shakes the bleachers, but Principal Richards shoots him a censorious glare over her glasses.

The warden's attention stays riveted on me. "Music is not a part of Volkranian culture."

Principal Richards smiles a bit too brightly and moves the card to the back of the stack.

"Dude, you pissed Scarface off," Sam whispers.

The scars on the warden's face have earned him that particularly uninventive nickname. And yes, he's scowling at me, but it's really no different than how he looked at me back in October. Until earlier that morning, I hadn't known it was going to be the fleet commandant visiting today. They'd been keeping it hush hush, not wanting a ton of news crews to show up. Fat chance.

All day, every day, the media covers the Volkranian invasion. The world is back in order, or so they tell us, but things still aren't back to normal. They never will be. Schools are in session —though we'll be attending classes throughout the summer to make up for the few months we lost last autumn when the human population suffered a total and complete meltdown. The economy is doing well, too, considering global commerce and trade had come to a screeching halt, and financial institutions stayed shut down for more than two weeks. But we're all good.

And we welcome the new species! Peaceful Settlement, everyone!

That's what the media tells us, and there are many, *many* people who embrace it. But there are independent Internet channels like the ones I recognize right now, set up on the track, spouting the total opposite opinion on YouTube. The Salvagers don't have a channel. Sam says it's because they don't want the aliens watching or knowing their plans. As if any of their "plans" could do anything to influence or harm the all-powerful Volkranians.

"Who do you think she is?" Sam whispers, his eyes stuck on the only female Volkranian out of five standing on the grass next to the stage. It's the pilot who flew me home, just after the first Volkron Six rocketed into outer space. Rowan trusted her, had called her a friend. And she's also found me in the crowd.

"Someone you don't want to mess with," I reply.

"She's looking at me," Sam says.

"Because you won't shut up," I reply, thankful he's arrogant enough to think the pilot is looking up here at *him*.

The pilot jerks her chin and sends a pointed glance off to the side of the bleachers. She then looks back at me. I follow her gaze to the cement block structure that houses the bathrooms. I meet her eyes again and frown. She looks again toward the outbuilding, and then discreetly slips away from the other Volkranians standing guard around the new fleet commandant. She heads toward the bathrooms.

Oh. *Oh!* A thrilling shiver races through me as I shift on the metal bench. She wants me to follow her. She wants to *talk* to me.

"I have to go to the bathroom," I whisper to Sam.

"What? *Now?* Scarface is still glaring at you with his freaky eyes."

"I either get up, or I puke all over you and Hannah," I whisper to Sam.

Hannah spins around, nostrils flaring. "Don't you dare puke on me."

"Just hurry up, okay?" Sam says. I frown at him. He's not usually so tense. This is a guy who does homework if he manages to get to it. A guy who lets his little sister paint his nails hot pink while he watches old movies.

"Don't get your panties in a twist," I say, standing up.

People shift their legs and knees as I make my way down the row, fielding murmured curse words and disbelieving glares along the way. I know what they're thinking: How *dare* I leave while the fleet commandant is speaking. It could be rude. It could be unacceptable. Could he, like, *execute* me for it?

If I was Volkranian? Most likely. But they haven't yet pushed their laws on humans. They haven't even really come down out of their cityships a whole lot. So far, the settlement has been moving glacially, and other than what happened in New York, pretty uneventful.

All I know is that right now, the pilot wants to talk to me. And after seven months of secretly craving the opportunity to speak to a Volkranian, any Volkranian, I'm not going to waste this opportunity.

I hurry down the side aisle of the bleachers as Principal Richards flips to another index card. "Do Volkranian women have two breas—" She chokes on the word. "*Mister Rivera!* That is *not* an appropriate question!"

One section of the bleachers erupts in laughter. Omar Rivera's section, I presume.

I hit the grass and turn toward the outbuilding. The girl's bathroom is on the opposite side, out of sight from the bleachers. I scoot around the cement block edge, the warden's voice blaring through the speakers. I eye the mint green door, take a breath, and push it open. It's dark inside. The vented, basement-type windows up near the ceiling only let in a little light. I wrinkle my nose; it smells like bleach mixed with old pee in here.

The principal's voice reaches through the bathroom walls. "In what ways was the planet Volkron similar to Earth? In what ways was it different?"

I step forward, waiting for the motion detector to sense me and trigger the fluorescent lights.

"Volkron was a terrestrial planet with a hydrosphere, and primary and secondary atmospheres, like Earth," the warden answers. I guess I should start thinking of him as fleet commandant now.

Only, Rowan is still the true fleet commandant. If he'd gotten onto the rescue core craft with me and about a hundred others, and abandoned his ship and his people, he would be the one speaking on that stage. But he hadn't. He'd stood tall and brave and sacrificed his chance for survival, all so he wouldn't leave his people to face their fate alone.

"Volkron is a highly volcanic planet, and water is scarce. There are only small pockets of land masses where life is permitted," the warden continues as I wave my arms, trying to catch the sensors.

A hand grasps my forearm. "Penelope."

I jerk my arm away and choke on a shriek.

"I disabled the lighting system in case another female human entered before you could arrive." The pilot's voice is soft, but it still echoes off the tiles. The lights then trip on, the fluorescent bulbs humming and clicking. The pilot pulls a hand-held gadget from the motion detector and slips it back into one of her suit's pockets.

She's still wearing the same blend of full-body jumpsuit and hard armor that she wore the last time I saw her. The exosuits Rowan and the other Volkranians had worn aren't seen in the news much anymore. The aliens have switched over to their under-layer jumpsuits. Rowan called them sec-suits, and they're much less intimidating than the black robotic exosuits—which have a laser weapon built into the right arm.

The pilot's serious gaze lands on me. She's just as tall as Rowan, at least six-five. I'd forgotten how big they are up close. Rowan had been as tall as an NBA player and thickly built. This pilot is similar. All Volkranians are taller, larger, and stronger, and from what Rowan explained, it's due to past genetic enhancements that evolved within Volkranian DNA.

"You're Rowan's friend," I say.

"Yes. I am now warden."

"Oh." I move out of the way as she goes to the door and stands against it, blocking any girl who might try to enter.

"What do you want?" I ask.

"The location device the fleet commandant gave to you."

I blink at the reference to Rowan as the fleet commandant, but then feel a sinking sensation in my stomach.

The location device. She has to be talking about the golden GPS disc Rowan gave me. But that had been in the privacy of Rowan's room on the cityship. I've kept the thumb-sized disc in the pocket of my jeans, or under my pillow, ever since. I rub it between my thumb and forefinger every night as I lie in bed trying to fall asleep. I never go anywhere without it, and that's because Rowan told me to keep it with me. *On my person.*

I slide back a step. "What device?"

Outside, the old warden is still speaking, and I catch a few words: Volkron. Contamination. Arid. Fruitless.

"The location device, Penelope. We require its return."

She stares at me with expectation, and even holds out her black-gloved hand, palm up. A thin vein of green runs through her brown eyes. It doesn't swirl into the iris the way Rowan's green and blue did. It's a resting band of green around each pupil. I can't continue to look into them. I shift my eyes to the long scar at her jaw, but then glance away from that too.

"I really don't know what you're talking about."

The golden disc is my last link to Rowan. Having it means I can at least keep a small part of him close. I don't want to give it up.

An unsteady round of applause reaches in through the cement blocks of the outbuilding. The pilot pitches her voice. "We have kept you under observation these last many months."

My hearing goes a bit muffled, and I stare at her lips. I'd been inside the original Volkron Six's control room where white-suited Volkranians watched fast-flipping screens of surveillance. I never considered any of the Volkranians aboard the new cityship would want to keep *me* under observation.

"We have seen you holding the device, Penelope."

Oh, crud.

I cross my arms and hold my ground without saying anything. Another question from Principal Richards fills the silence: "Are the Volkranians eager to settle on the ground amongst humans?"

I'd like to hear the answer to that one too, but the pilot takes a step in my direction, her armored chest now looming in front of my face.

"You were of interest to Rowan," she says. I meet her eyes, surprised. Rowan isn't his true Volkranian name, and the other Volkranians had seemed offended that I called him that.

"He was a brother to me," she continues. "Because of that, I offer to protect you."

I keep staring at her as my mind spins. Volkranians are cold and rigid. They're uninviting and severe. They're our new neighbors and overlords, and no one likes them. But at this second, with *this* Volkranian, I experience what I did with

Rowan: a confusing warmth that makes me feel like there's a balloon inflating in my chest.

"Protect me from what?"

She lets out a long breath. "There could soon be, for reasons I cannot explain, a danger in carrying Volkranian technology."

I'm not ready to admit the location device is in my right jeans pocket, but she definitely has my attention.

"Why?"

"I already said I cannot explain the reason."

I've been careful with the disc. My mom knows everything about Rowan—how we met in the wastewater treatment plant, how he'd taken me prisoner aboard Volkron Six, how he'd become honor bound to me and saved my life, and how he'd admitted to caring about me after he'd defeated his treasonous father—but she doesn't know I have the disc.

I've prepared to pass it off as a fancy guitar pick found on a sidewalk in case Sam or Hayden or my mom happen to get a glance of it.

"What kind of danger?" I press.

"Mortal," the pilot answers without hesitation.

My right jeans pocket promptly gains twenty pounds.

"Who's the danger coming from, humans or Volkranians?"

"I cannot say," she repeats, her patience wearing thin. "I need you to trust me. The technology will make you a target. I will also require the return of the weapon I gave you."

She'd given me a sword for protection when she'd dropped me off at home, back in October. I stored it under my mattress and have actually felt safer with it there.

I clench my hands into fists. I was a target before. I'd been Rowan's weakness, though we'd only known each another for two days. I'm still not sure how or why I grew to trust him so explicitly, or why he chose to protect me and help me the way he had. It had just...happened.

"Does your name translate into English?" I want to trust this pilot the way Rowan did, but not knowing something as basic as her name makes it difficult.

"It does." Her dark eyebrows pull together, perhaps in surprise. "It translates into a handful of English words. Ember, ash, coal, and cinder."

The remnants of a fire.

"I like Ash," I say.

The corner of her mouth twitches. "If you will give me the location device—"

But her next words are devoured by a roaring sound, then a rocking explosion. The force of it trembles up through the floor and shakes my bones as I crouch and cover my head. With a shattering crash, the panel of fluorescent lights falls onto the sinks and countertop. Ceiling plaster rains down on top of our heads, and I realize what's just happened.

A bomb. Someone has detonated a freaking bomb.

CHAPTER TWO

My ears ring as I lie on the floor, a sharp chime drilling into my head—and then the screams break through. My heart cements to my ribs, and I stop breathing, but Ash takes my arm and snaps me out of my stupor.

"Hurry!" She hauls me to my feet and rushes out of the bathroom, back toward the staging area. My feet flop along and my ears ache. Maybe I've blown an eardrum. But concern for that evaporates as a crowd of students rushes through the wall of smoke, screaming and crying. A girl with blood all over her face knocks into my shoulder as she runs by us, her expression a mask of fear. More come, stumbling away from the bleachers, pushing past one another.

Ash keeps her hand on my arm and pulls me through the tide of people moving away from the football field and bleachers. The staging has collapsed, one side of it smashed onto the grass. The podium where the warden and Principal Richards had been standing has fallen forward, onto the track. Principal Richards is on her side, one white-heeled pump gone, her foot bare. The warden lifts her to her feet, her hand pressed to her bleeding temple. Cameras swarm the stage, news reporters shouting orders to their crews.

"Pen!"

Sam's voice reaches through the chaos, though I can't see him. I open my mouth to shout back, but I only cough on acrid smoke.

"The transport is critically damaged," the warden says to Ash as we reach him and Principal Richards.

Ash's grip tightens around my upper arm as another swarm of people appears out of the smoke. The students and teachers are limping past, the lanes on the track congested, but a half dozen or so people are pushing through, shouting a chant I recognize: "*Crush, defeat, reclaim! Crush, defeat, reclaim!*"

It's the Salvager's motto. Their fight song.

"Commandant, we must go," Ash says as Principal Richards kicks off her remaining shoe and runs from the collapsed staging without acknowledging me.

"Another transport is en route," the warden replies. His silver irises settle on me for a spare moment before shifting back toward the oncoming mob of mostly men, and a few women. They look like they could be computer programmers and Starbucks baristas, but I know very well what they're capable of.

They've been targeting both Volkranians and pro-Peaceful Settlement humans to prove that they're willing to do anything to drive the aliens out. They're radicals, and apparently, blowing up a high school assembly is on their list of acceptable action.

"Penelope." Ash lets go of my arm. "Run."

But I can't move. I stand there frozen and unblinking as the angry Salvagers close in. They're holding baseball bats and tire irons, and a few have weapons in their hands. One raises an automatic pistol, turned sideways, Hollywood-movie gangster style. The idiot pulls the trigger. Ash throws herself on top of me, crushing me into the grass. It feels like being flattened by a steel beam.

"No!" Sam, wherever he is, screams as a few more pops of gunfire erupts.

A blast of wind presses down over us, whipping up the odor of dirt and smoke and tar. *A transport.* A white flash sweeps side-to-side in front of us. The laser sears a long line into the track and grass and then swings back again, like a pendulum, creating a barrier between us and the oncoming mob.

"Stay down!" Ash shouts in my ear, her chest rumbling.

And then the weight of Ash's body is gone. I stay on the grass, covering my head, and twist to watch as she and the warden disappear through the open door of a transport. Then with a soft whir, the transport rockets into the sky.

"Pen!" Sam grabs my shoulders and rolls me over. "Those goddamned assholes—are you hurt?"

"No," I say, my voice loud in my head. I turn to see the mob of Salvagers already running away from the smoking line burned into the track and field, screaming and howling with pride. "No. I'm...I'm okay."

I cling to Sam's arm as he helps me to my feet. In the field, the transport the warden and Ash arrived in less than a half an hour before is charred, the nautilus-shaped body dented. Nearby is a huge black crater in the grass.

"I'm going to kill them," Sam mutters, his eyes on the crater, too. Wailing police sirens make my eardrums pulsate. "Let's get the hell out of here."

"Wait..." I look around, my head spinning. "Is anyone hurt? We should help—"

"Help is coming," Sam says as ambulance lights flicker between trees lining the football field, "but we need to go."

He leads me around cameras and news reporters, who are shouting into their phones and microphones. He averts his face from the cameras as I stumble beside him, my legs like putty, my head and ears still a muffled bubble of high-pitched ringing. He doesn't want them broadcasting his image.

"Sam." I'm breathless as we reach the parking lot. "Tell me what's happening."

"In the car," he says, manually unlocking the old Volvo he drives us to school in every day. Sometimes I drive too, but right now my arms are shaking, and my left ear is killing.

"Where are we going?" I ask as soon as we're on the road.

Soon, news of the explosion will reach my mom, at work at the temporary hospital in Eastham. I can't call or text her to let her know we're okay—we weren't allowed to bring our bags or phones out to the bleachers for the assembly, so they're stuck in the school, in our lockers.

"I know you hate it there, but I have to go," he answers.

A surge of anger licks through me. "Diesel's place? Sam, come on. You saw them!"

The Salvagers are anarchists. Radicals. And Diesel is their leader. "They're the ones behind the explosion—can't you see that?" I ask.

Sam locks his jaw shut as police cars and ambulances zoom past us, toward the high school. They're vintage and look like they belong on the set of a 1970s Burt Reynolds movie. Last fall, the EMP, or the "radioflash" as some people call it, had killed the automotive industry. All vehicles built after the 1980s with computers as part of their engine make-up were destroyed. The only cars that weren't affected were the ones that had been built prior to the computer age. Thankfully, Sam's father's old garage and the junkyard behind it had a number of old cars rotting away, useless. Fixing them had been hard and finding parts had been tougher, but people paid Sam well for what he offered. The factories are churning out new cars now, but people are skeptical. What if another EMP comes? What if they become useless again?

Sam grips the steering wheel, his fingers kneading the leather. "Are you sure you're not hurt?"

My ear is nothing compared to what other people might have suffered. "I'm okay. Are you?"

He makes a sharp turn to the left. "Forget about me. If they'd shot you... Jesus, Pen, what the hell were you doing standing next to that Volkranian?"

For the last several minutes, I'd completely forgotten about meeting Ash in the bathroom. I reach into my pocket and touch the golden disc. She'd said I could be in danger because of it. Did the bomb have anything to do with it?

"I don't know," I tell Sam, hating that I have to lie. "I got lost in the smoke. I was just...there."

"You need to stay away from them," he says as he turns down another street without using his turn signal or the brakes.

"She helped me, Sam," I reply, teeth gritted. He sounds like me, all the times I've told him to stay away from Diesel and his followers.

He glances across the front seat. He doesn't let his anger show all that much, though I know it's there, simmering underneath the easy, relaxed front he usually puts on. Mostly, the show is for his kid sister. Hayden is only eight. She has nightmares about the aliens almost every night. Sam tries to act casual about the invasion, using humor and indifference to show her that the aliens aren't anything to be scared of. It's a pretty good con. Sometimes I almost fall for it, too.

He pulls into an empty parking spot along Blake Street and cuts the engine. We both look through the windshield at the front of Inkopolis for a few silent moments. It's more than just a tattoo shop.

"Diesel's here," Sam replies.

I know. The closed sign hanging on the door is slanted to the left, signaling his presence inside.

"It's stupid coming here. What if the police know where Salvager headquarters is? What if they've just been waiting for the right moment to raid?" I ask.

The Salvagers aren't my crowd. I only go to the meetings with Sam every now and again because I feel as if I should. He's letting my mom and me live with him after all. He's passionate about taking back our city—our world—from the Volkranians, and the Salvagers think they're going to be able to do it. But sitting through these pointless, underground meetings during the evening, listening to a combination of ex-military, business-types, and college students complain about aliens, and hatching lame plans for an attempted storming of the cityship, just makes me want to grind my teeth and scream.

However, there's another faction of Salvagers. They don't complain—they act. These are the ones I try to stay away from. They're the ones we saw today at the high school. Even Sam doesn't want anything to do with them, and thankfully, they don't show up at Inkopolis very often.

"Stay in the car if you want," he says, and then opens his door and gets out.

Like that's going to happen.

I get out and follow him toward the narrow alley that leads to the back door of the tattoo shop. A dumpster sits as a kind of partition between the street and the back door. Sam raps on the hollow metal door. When an answering rap comes back, Sam says the password clearly: "Fried Pickles."

Yeah. It's *that* sophisticated.

The door cracks open. A guy named Henry sticks out his long, thin nose, covered in a spray of freckles and pimples. "What's up, man? Come on in."

Henry pulls open the door, and Sam gestures for me to

enter first. I stall out, shocked at how packed the back room of the tattoo shop is. At least a dozen people, maybe more, stand around the small room, the walls papered with tattoo designs, 1950s pin-up girls, and magazine cutouts of muscle cars. Sam and I cram shoulders to fit into the room.

"Streeter," Diesel calls out. The local Salvage faction leader is big; I suspect from lifting at the gym and downing protein shakes. He's covered in his craft, with full sleeves of ink and a heavily-tatted neck too. He wears a bandana around his balding head and frayed jeans. His eyes narrow in on me and Sam. "Wasn't expecting you."

The others quiet down and turn their attention our way. I recognize Henry, but the faces of these Salvagers aren't familiar. They look like a biker gang or Crossfit fanatics. All brawn and height, and leather and denim. Their scowls are almost cliché.

One guy catches my attention. He's perhaps the largest of the group, with white-blond hair and pale blue eyes. He wears a black leather jacket and a pair of motorcycle goggles around his neck, and he's looking at me with an intensity the others don't have.

"We were at the school," Sam says. "What the hell went wrong? The transport was supposed to be hit with a guided missile, not by a bomb planted on the twenty-yard line. The bleachers were full."

I rip my attention from the blond guy with the goggles and stare at Sam. His words punch, landing hard in the bottom of my throat. He'd *known* about the planned attack?

"And then they opened fire. There were still *people* in the way," Sam continues, his voice rising.

Diesel turns his back and goes to the fridge. "I know, man. It was a setback. Things are being handled."

He'd known. *Sam had known.* He planned to just watch as

the transport carrying the new fleet commandant and the other Volkranians blew up in the sky?

"A *setback*?" Sam shouts. "They nearly shot Pen."

Diesel looks at me now. They all do. I lift my chin and try not to look blown over by what Sam has just revealed.

Diesel grabs a couple of beers from the fridge and extends them to Sam and me. "I'm sorry. Are you okay?"

I reject the beer. So does Sam, and Diesel shrugs before setting them down onto an ink cart.

"I'm fine," I say for the billionth time. But Sam won't be. I can't wait to get out of this place and beat him senseless with whatever object I can find in the alley.

I'm tempted to storm outside right now, but I stay where I am and school my expression. I don't want to appear angry. The other guys in the room are looking on with a tension that borders on dangerous.

"Glad to hear that, Pen," Diesel says, and he sounds like he means it. But he doesn't care. Not really. He's a talker. A charmer. He says what he needs to in order to get what he wants. I guess he's even been successful in convincing Sam to attack the Volkranians. A guided *missile*? How had they gotten their hands on that kind of weapon?

"Listen, Streeter. We've got a mess to figure out, okay? And we have to be careful. There were a shitload of people filming there. My crew could end up being identified."

"Then maybe they shouldn't have tried to attack the Volkranians like some street mob," I say, fury rising.

Diesel bristles, and Sam's hand touches down on my hip. He tries to pull me back, closer to him, but I shift away. I can't believe he's actually a part of this attack.

"They weren't given those orders," Diesel replies, his jaw tight. "They'll be dealt with."

The others nod and murmur their agreement. Diesel jerks

his chin toward the back door. "You should probably clear out before they show up."

I go cold. They're coming *here*? They would recognize me as the one standing with the female Volkranian. Even Sam had been suspicious. The Salvagers who had been at the blast could easily accuse me of being a sympathizer. Sam glances at me. He knows as well as I do that lately, sympathizers have a way of ending up dead.

He takes my hand, nods toward Diesel and the others, and heads toward the back door. I glance over my shoulder. Goggles Guy is still eyeing me. I don't know him. Have definitely never seen him before. But that stare...it's too forward and intense to mean nothing. Does he know something?

As Sam and I leave through the back door of Inkopolis, I remember what Ash said before the bomb detonated: that Volkranian technology would make me a target.

Being on the other end of Goggles Guy's stare had definitely made me feel like one.

CHAPTER THREE

THE SECOND THE back door shuts and locks, I tear my hand from Sam's. "How could you?"

"Pen, I know I should have said something—"

I turn my back to him and rush for the mouth of the alley. "Don't." I cross the street and head for the car. "Not here."

I still feel eyes on me—from inside the tattoo shop *and* up in the sky.

"I'll explain."

"Shut it, Sam."

He catches up to me and takes my arm, forcing me to stop in the middle of the street. There's no traffic, only distant sirens and the chop of helicopter blades.

"If I had known how everything would go down—"

"People may have been killed," I say, my voice pitched barely above a whisper.

Sam closes his eyes and breathes in. He sways a little on his feet, guilt slashing across his face.

"You *have* to get out," I whisper, chancing a look at the shop windows. They're blacked out with dark purple paint, but I know Diesel scraped off a few peepholes a while back so he could look outside. "They're dangerous."

Sam opens his eyes, and that hard, obstinate shine is back. "They're the only ones doing *anything* to try and stop the aliens."

"Salvagers are terrorists." My voice is getting louder, and Sam steers me toward the car again. "Terrorists set off bombs in public spaces, not the heroes."

He opens the Volvo's passenger side door for me. "This is a new world. Rules need to be broken and re-written—"

"Did Diesel feed that line to you? Did he make you memorize it? Does it make you feel okay about organized chaos?"

"I don't feel okay about any of it!" He checks over his shoulder. "They screwed up today—"

"Did you help plant the bomb?"

I have to know. If he did, I can't live with him anymore. I have no idea where my mom and I will go, but I refuse to live under the same roof as a fanatic.

"No. I didn't help—I promise," he adds when I narrow my eyes, digging for the truth. "There was supposed to be a rocket launcher on the roof of a nearby house. I gave Diesel a good idea for where his guy could stand for a clear line of sight. That's all."

My eyes sting as tears well up. That's *all*? "Yeah, well, I guess that's enough to still be guilty as hell."

He bites back a retort and shakes his head. "You don't get it."

"What exactly do you think you can accomplish?" I ask, ignoring the passenger seat when he gestures to it. "Their technology, their weapons, their intelligence...it all tops ours, exponentially. They could have wiped out mankind, but they didn't. They're here to stay. Shouldn't we be trying to find a way to live with them instead?"

Sam turns his shoulders to block me from view of the shop windows. "Keep your voice down."

"So I don't sound like a sympathizer?" I walk away from the Volvo and start down the sidewalk. "Or maybe Diesel and the other Salvagers just don't like it when people think for themselves."

"Where are you going?"

I keep walking, still shivering despite the bright sun and cloudless sky. "The hospital. My mom is probably worried."

"I can drive you," he says, sounding exasperated. Good. At least now I'm not the only one.

"It's a few blocks. I'll walk." I don't turn around. Sometimes, he pushes my buttons the way I imagine a brother might. Other times, like when he put his hand on my hip inside the tattoo shop, I feel claustrophobic for other reasons.

He's held my hand a few times. Hugged me. Kissed my forehead once when I knocked it against one of the lifts in his garage. The way my body leaps under his fingers bothers me though. I don't want it to be *Sam* who makes me feel that way.

I turn the corner and hear the rattling ignition of the Volvo. It's almost time for him to pick up Hayden from her school. Kids don't walk home alone anymore like they used to. I hardly see anyone riding bikes or skateboards. Then again, spring has barely started, so it could have nothing at all to do with the aliens. Time will tell, I guess, but things do feel more... restricted. Careful.

The Sovereign made apologies for the destruction and deaths in New York City last October. He'd punished his own people. And the fact that no other Volkranian-occupied city suffered great death or damage made his case easier to plead. Humans had rioted, of course, and panicked, but outside of one fleet commandant's rogue actions, the Volkranians have been as peaceful as they claim to be.

The approximately thirty thousand dead and missing in New York City and surrounding areas cannot be erased from memory, though. The number is likely higher than thirty thousand, but people stopped counting after that. There didn't seem to be any point to keep specific tally. After a while, I stopped feeling the pangs of anguish when the death toll rose. My mind couldn't handle it. Neither could my heart. Especially since, with every passing day, it seemed my dad was one of the thousands missing. So, my mind and heart had just sort of...turned off.

I've stopped thinking about my best friend Tana and the other students and teachers from Alton High that were killed. I can't let myself think about them, not without wanting to fold up and tuck myself away forever. And not just because they died...but because I don't absolutely hate the people who killed them.

I don't want revenge. And that doesn't make sense.

It's a new world, Sam said. He's at least right about that.

I turn into the hospital's parking lot and start for the registration tent. The original hospital, ruined beyond repair in October, had since been demolished, and a new one is slowly being built in the same location. My mom and all the other hospital employees spent the better part of the winter in what looks like a tent city, the interconnected weather-proof tents housing everything from urgent care to pediatrics, including my mom's department, radiology.

They know me here, more so than before. I used to go home after school, but now I usually go with Sam to pick up Hayden, and then the three of us come to the hospital to meet my mom. There's also free food at the cafeteria tent, so that's another incentive.

Linda at registration catches sight of me and waves me

through the line. I apologize to the people who've been waiting and scoot behind the desk.

"Are you hurt? Your mom's been calling all around trying to find out if you were admitted," she says, her eyes inspecting me. She's nice, and always has some kind of cartoony sticker or cheap toy for Hayden.

"I'm okay," I answer, then after taking a breath, ask, "Was anyone badly injured?"

The corners of her mouth turn down, and I know the answer.

"No deaths. But there's a boy in surgery who's most likely going to lose his leg."

Oh god. I think I'm going to be sick. Linda sees it and grasps my hand. "Go on back. Nic will be so relieved to see you."

I nod and move toward the back door of the tent. It connects to the next tent by a short, tube-like corridor and a flimsy door. In each corridor and tent, the whir of HVAC systems continuously clean the air. A boy is losing his leg. Sam's not responsible. But he kind of is. Which, strangely, makes *me* feel a little responsible, even though I know it's stupid to think that.

"Hi, Pen," a doctor my mom knows says as we pass each other in the tube between orthopedics and endocrinology. "Glad to see you're okay."

"Thanks," I tell her, but don't stop to talk.

I hate that my mom is worrying about me, wondering if I've been hurt. Not knowing what happened to Dad—and coming to the realization that he probably isn't coming home—has been tough on her. On both of us. We're not the same without him, just like we weren't the same after my little brother died a few years ago. Losing Ollie to a distracted driver had made my mom way more protective than she'd ever been before. Now, losing Dad too has taken another huge toll on her. She's always so uncertain these days and apprehensive.

I enter through the flimsy door marked as Radiology and find a packed waiting room. Two pregnant women, a girl in a leg cast, and an older couple glance away from the television screen sitting on a table to see who's joined their party. I smile half-heartedly and see the News 9 reporter on screen, and Alton High's football field in the backdrop.

I approach the desk where Pauline, dressed in green scrubs and a white turtleneck, sits at one of the new computers that flooded the world over the winter. They're supposedly EMP-proof. Pauline closes her eyes and blows out a long breath.

"There you are," she says, reaching for the phone. She pushes a button and waits for my mom to pick up. "She's here."

Pauline hangs up, and points to her computer screen. "Have you seen this yet?"

I glance over the desk and see the news coverage streaming live on her screen.

"No," I say. "I don't need to. I was there."

And I want to forget every moment of it. Well...not every moment. Talking to Ash had been like letting out a breath I'd been holding for far too long.

The door to the radiology rooms bursts open and my mom comes sailing through. Her dark hair is piled on top of her head, and she's wearing the eggplant purple scrubs I like better than any other color she has.

"Thank God," she says, meeting me halfway around the desk and wrapping me in a hug. She's an inch shorter than I am with finer bone structure, so I don't squeeze her too tightly. "You're okay?" She pulls back. "Sam, too?"

I nod, but don't trust myself to say anything. She knows when I'm angry. My voice gets high pitched. And yes, right now, I'm still furious with him.

"Nic. Pen. You want to watch this," Pauline says, and I follow my mom behind the desk. The news is replaying smoky footage, and the camera is shaking. I peer closely at the screen, trying to make out what I'm seeing. Kids rushing past the camera lens, smoke, the collapsed staging area, the warden crouching to help Principal Richards stand, her single white pump hanging off her foot.

And then I see it. I'm hazy through the smoke, but I still see me being dragged into view, Ash's hand wrapped around my arm. Seconds later, Ash is tackling me to the ground as gunfire pops. The camera angle swings, and it focuses on the group of Salvagers. I can't make out faces, but someone who can pause the shaky footage and clarify it will definitely be able to determine who they are.

"Oh my God, that's one of them," Pauline says. In the waiting area, the others have been viewing the same footage. They glance over at me, eyes wide as they make the connection. My cheeks start to burn.

Pauline swivels in her chair and stares up at me. "She had you. She was touching you. A *Volkranian* was touching you."

My mom's hand on my forearm squeezes gently. I don't know if it's a warning or not. I try to remember if she's ever said anything about Pauline being pro-Peaceful Settlement, or more anti-alien leaning, but can't.

"She was trying to help," I say.

Pauline snorts and gestures to the live coverage on her screen. It's replaying the last fifteen-second clip. "She body slammed you onto the grass."

"To shield me from bullets," I reply, starting to shake again. "They can't penetrate their suits, remember?"

I want to go home. I don't want these people staring at me, and I don't want to think about Ash or her request to give her the golden disc.

"She protected you," my mom says.

I nod and see more questions in the barely noticeable arch

of her eyebrow. *What were you doing with a Volkranian? Does this have anything to do with Rowan?* My mom is no fool. She's avoided speaking about Rowan and what happened last October, but she certainly hasn't forgotten.

Pauline is gawping at her computer screen again. "She's enormous! My word." She hushes her voice and turns away from the waiting room. "Did she say anything to you? What did she feel like?"

What did she *feel* like? What does Pauline expect me to say —that she was slimy and the head that came out of her chest nearly ate me?

"She told me to stay down," I answer, ready to get away from her and the rest of the patients, all still watching and listening. "And she felt...heavy."

My mom squeezes my arm again and cuts off Pauline before she can ask another question. "I'm leaving to take Pen home."

She can do that. Since October, my mom has practically been running this department. The head radiologist had packed up his family and fled Eastham immediately after the attacks, and in the following months, the numbers of employees had dwindled. My mom is one of the last holdouts, so she pretty much gets to make her own hours. They're lucky she likes to work a lot, if only to spend less time thinking about my dad.

My mom collects her things, and we walk through the maze of tubes toward registration, each of us silent. I feel like I'm holding my breath, too.

The moment we clear the lobby tent, she turns to me. "Okay. Spill."

CHAPTER FOUR

I EXHALE and tell her everything, from Ash's request to give her the GPS tracker and the sword, to the bomb and the Salvagers. I don't mention Sam's involvement though, or our trip to Inkopolis after. She would flip if she knew about that. She might even insist we find a new place to stay. I don't want to leave Hayden high and dry. She's come to depend on us, I think.

"Wait—Rowan gave you something?" my mom asks as we cross a road.

I know that I should have told her about it, but the disc had felt special and private...it had been something I had kept just for myself.

I reach into my pocket and show it to her. She stops to look but doesn't move to touch it. "It's GPS?"

"He gave it to me when he thought he was still going to be up there," I say, pointing toward the egg in the sky.

I just can't take that cityship seriously.

"And he wanted to know where you were," she guesses.

I nod and put the disc back in my pocket. She doesn't ask why I never told her. Maybe she's already figured it out.

She starts to walk again. "So, you think this Volkranian woman will be coming back to get it?"

"She said keeping it would make me a target, though she didn't explain why or how."

So yeah, I suppose we can count on seeing Ash again sometime soon. Maybe even tonight. Unless the bomb had unnerved her, and she'd decided to shirk her vow of protection. Though, she doesn't seem the shirking type.

"Do what she asks," my mom says, surprising me with her firm tone. "If she wants the disc, give it to her. I want you safe."

She takes my arm as we cross another street, toward Sam's garage. It's an industrial type of business area, with no homes or residential streets nearby. It's quiet at night, at least. Sometimes too quiet, and it makes me feel as if the world has gone totally post-apocalyptic.

"I will," I tell her, and I realize it's the truth. I'll give Ash the disc. Rowan is gone. Holding on to this little thumb-sized disc is pathetic. It doesn't help me remember Rowan any better. I can do that all on my own, and I do...often.

Sam's Volvo is parked out front of Streeter's Garage when the building comes into view. It's run down, with a gray-painted cinder block exterior and an old, stamped metal sign swinging from a pole. Above the garage is the two-bedroom apartment where we're all living. It's cramped, and I've been sleeping in a pantry, but I can't complain.

Sam had tried to insist I take his room and that he would sleep in the food-packed, makeshift fourth bedroom. I hadn't felt right about it though, so I bunked in the pantry with cans of peas and corn, bags of flour and sugar and pasta, and rice and beans. I would lie in there at night deciding what we could eat the next day. It was also warm when the heat was on, the pipes running right underneath the lowest shelf. It all worked out. For now, at least.

One of the garage bay doors is rolled open and the sound of metal hammering on metal clangs out into the air. We walk into the scent of oil and gasoline and rust and find Sam elbow deep in an old Chevrolet's front end. He glances up, his attention immediately fixing on me.

"Is Hayden upstairs?" my mom asks. "She isn't watching television, is she?"

She doesn't want Hayden to see the news coverage. Bombs and aliens tackling me to the ground would give her even more nightmares than usual.

Sam shakes his head. "She's in her room, playing."

I follow my mom to the back corner of the shop to the stairs leading to the apartment. Sam's eyes follow me, his forehead crinkling. He wants me to hang back.

"I'll be up in a few minutes," I tell my mom. She glances at Sam and nods tightly. For the first time, I wonder if she's been catching drift of Sam's changing interest in me.

She doesn't say anything, though, and climbs the staircase to the apartment above. The door up there is open, probably so Sam can hear Hayden calling if she needs him. My mom leaves it open.

I walk toward the Chevrolet, tapping my fingers along a metal table covered in parts and tools. I kick my feet through a pile of cat litter. It's not specifically for Mister Mister, though that doesn't stop my cat from using it. Sam just spreads the litter over oil and grease spills to absorb them. Every now and th

en, however, he finds a little something extra in the piles, compliments of Mister Mister.

Sam usually has the radio on, but today it's silent.

"No one died, but some kid is losing his leg," I say, my voice echoing off the high ceiling.

Sam braces his hands against the car and leans forward, his

shoulders rounding as he drops his head. I can't see his face, but I can guess what he's feeling: a stomach-load of guilt.

He isn't a bad guy. He isn't cruel. He's just angry—he lost his parents, his little sister lives in fear, and he's taken in two strangers. My mom and I try not to be burdens, but I know he feels responsible for us.

"I can't get out, Pen." Sam pushes off the car and crosses his arms. "I know too much about their organization. Their plans."

I know. I wish he'd never gotten in so deep.

Sam walks toward the table and grabs a roll of blue shop towels. He rips off a length and wipes at his black-coated fingers. He leaves the streaks of black and deep red grease along his forearm, though.

"You're right, though. I know you're right," he whispers, unable to look at me as he rubs each finger. "They're not heroes. I'm not, either."

"Sam—"

"I'm not a hero, Pen, and I never intended to be one," he says, louder now. He crumples the shop towel and tosses it onto the table. "I'm willing to fight dirty if it means making a difference. If it means taking back our freedom."

I could argue that we're still free. We aren't imprisoned somewhere, or under attack. We're working, going to school, coming and going without having to answer to anyone. But the tightness of our lives, the constant worry and fear and not knowing what's going to happen next... these things are a prison, too.

"Then maybe you can change the Salvagers," I say. It's far fetched but I can't give up. "Lead them to be something more than hot-headed conspiracy theorists and low-budget terrorists."

Sam shakes his head. "Diesel's their leader here."

"If I can see through his bull, other people can, too. Give them an alternative."

He's still shaking his head, but a smile is starting to stretch across his cheeks.

"What?" I ask.

Sam stops and stares at me. "Would you follow that alternative?"

That's a serious question.

We've only known one another for a short while, but it's been an intense short while. Living close like this has also kicked our "getting-to-know-you" phase into overdrive. We'd been pushed together because of need. The way he's looking at me right now, his eyes drifting to my mouth and then my hair, as if he wants to touch the dark strands, looks and feels like need, too.

A puff ball of gray fur leaps onto the shop table and lets out a motor-like purr. Sam laughs at Mister Mister and scratches between his ears.

"Or do you think I'm just another hot-headed conspiracy theorist who can't think for himself?" Sam asks, glancing over at me.

He's many things, but not a brainless follower. I pick up a wrench. It's heavy, and I feel the grease on the steel handle before I see it.

"You're devoted," I say, reaching for the blue shop towel. Sam grabs it first and comes closer. He takes my hand and finds the streak of grease on my palm.

"I am. Not just to the Salvagers though. To Hayden. To you and your mom." He rubs the towel against my palm in slow strokes. "You're the people I need to look out for first."

He takes another step closer, until his feet frame mine. I trace oil and the almond scented soap he uses to wash up with every morning.

"Pen." He lets go of my hand and his fingers coast along my

cheek, his thumb and forefinger hooking the tip of my chin. He nudges it, lifting my mouth.

I should just let Sam kiss me. Maybe his mouth, his hands, would snuff out the fire I feel whenever I think of Rowan. I only knew Rowan for two days. I've known Sam for seven months. My feelings for him should be stronger and deeper.

"I want you with me. You don't have to come to the Salvager meetings anymore, but I want you with me."

Sam's eyes haven't strayed from my lips.

Oh, crap. "Don't."

It doesn't break his concentration. "Why not?"

Is it just me or are his lips inching closer? "It would change things."

"I'm okay with that." His fingers leave my chin and curl around to the base of my neck.

Sam's lips touch mine for one sparking moment. Long enough for my stomach to twist and my mind to race.

He's human. He's like me. He's my kind.

I pull my lips from his. "Stop."

He doesn't move away. "I know you feel something for me, Pen. This isn't a one-sided attraction."

He's right, and I hate that he's right. I *am* attracted to him. At least my body is. But my mind and body seem so disconnected lately.

Sam's lips touch mine again. *This isn't right. I don't want this.* I press my palms against his chest and push, twisting my head away. At that moment, Mister Mister yowls and hisses, leaping off the table. I stare after my cat, curious about what scared him, and see someone standing in the open bay.

"*Sam,*" I whisper, and this time, he takes the hint. He turns to see our visitor.

It's the Salvager from Inkopolis. Goggles Guy. The pair of goggles is still hanging around his neck. Motorcycle goggles? I hadn't heard the sound of a bike engine approaching. Then again, Sam had been trying to kiss me.

"Hey," Sam says, though it's a question more than a greeting.

The Salvager walks into the garage. His pale blue eyes roam inquisitively over the Chevrolet. He lifts his gloved hand and touches a few of the air hoses and power drills hanging down from the ceiling.

"You want something?" Sam asks after a few seconds of silence.

The Salvager keeps walking toward the table where Sam and I are standing, his attention riveted to other things, as if he's never spent time in a garage. Sam shifts his footing and turns to face him, moving slightly to block me.

"What are you doing here?" Sam asks. He's clearly unnerved and getting pissed.

The Salvager smiles and raises his hand. There's a small bottle tucked into his palm. A spray of mist jets out of it, hitting Sam in the face. He coughs once—and then goes down.

"Sam!" I jump forward to catch him before he hits his head on the cement floor, but the Salvager beats me to it. He deftly lowers Sam the rest of the way to the floor before standing up and extending his hand to me.

"Penelope, I need you to come with me."

I narrow my gaze. No one calls me Penelope.

The hair on my arms prickle and stand up straight.

No one except Rowan and the other Volkranians.

I stare between Sam's limp body and the Salvager. "What the hell did you just do?"

"He will be fine. But I require your cooperation."

His choice of words leaves me even more on edge. So formal. So *polite.* I check his neck under the pair of motorcycle goggles. It's all skin. No translator collar. He isn't a Volkranian.

They can't speak English without them. At least, at first they couldn't. Maybe they've learned our language by now?

The heavy wrench I'd picked up earlier is still on the table at my side. I grab it and hold it up as I would a weapon.

"I'm not going anywhere with you." I back up a step. My heels slide to an abrupt halt. I can't go up to the apartment. My mom and Hayden are there. If this guy is dangerous—and I'm thinking he is—I can't lead him to them.

I shift to the left. There's a rear door that leads into a back alleyway bordered by an industrial chain link fence. A break in the fence opens up into a massive junkyard, a few football fields in length and width. If I can get in there and start to run, I could lose him.

The Salvager follows me. He doesn't lunge or try to spray my face with the stuff he's taken Sam down with. He simply walks.

"We do not mean you harm, Penelope. We only seek an audience with Prince Torrin."

Half of my attention is on what he's saying. The other half gets stuck on an air compressor hose hanging by the rear door, where Sam has a tire changer. I've watched him use the air compressor a number of times and even caught a gust of it in my eyes once when Sam had been fooling around. A high-pressure gust of air might not hurt this guy, but I have another idea in mind.

"Stay away from me," I say, my voice warbling as I brandish the wrench.

He takes one more step. *Close enough.*

I drop the wrench and crouch, scooping up one of the piles of kitty litter over an oil spill. On my way back up, I grab the air compressor hose, pull back the nozzle, and hold up my other hand, palm flat. A burst of compressed air sprays the litter right into his eyes.

He shields his face, but not fast enough. He twists away, rubbing at his eyes and hissing under his breath. I drop the hose and burst through the rear door, into the back alley, and I make a run for the gap in the fence. The junkyard is a maze of scrap metal and cars rusting into the earth, heaps of broken brick and stone and wood. It's a computer graveyard now, too.

It feels like I'm moving in slow motion, and it's amazing he hasn't tackled me by the time I get through the opening. Kind of ironic that Goggles hadn't been wearing his goggles when he'd needed them most. But now isn't the time to think about irony. I almost trip over a couple of stacked tires, but I save myself and keep running into the junkyard. He's behind me, his feet pounding the ground, his leather jacket creaking and rustling as he gives chase.

I keep running, relieved I'm drawing him away from the apartment, but worried about Sam. And what the hell had the Salvager been talking about? Prince Torrin? I let it go. Confusion will only slow me down.

I dart around the obstacles in front of me—an overturned filing cabinet, a pile of computer monitors, a pyramid of cinderblocks, a Leaning Tower of Michelins, clear plastic trash bags filled with aluminum cans.

For a split second, I have hope that I'll be able to make it to the rear exit of the junkyard—if there even *is* a rear exit. But his hulking figure emerges out from behind the tower of tires, and I slam into him full bore, chin first. I topple back and land on the ground, my vision blurring. My wrist smacks onto something hard—a length of bent and mangled metal pipe. I grasp it and hold it in front of me.

"Back off!" I try for my most menacing tone, but I'm breathless so it comes out more like an angry Theodore from *Alvin and the Chipmunks*.

"Prince Torrin will come for you, and so, you will come with me," he replies.

I dig my heels into the packed dirt and push backward. "I don't think so."

"We seek only to reveal the truth to him. My orders are to deliver you unharmed. However, if you resist, I have the authority to render you unconscious."

"Deliver me where? To who?" I shove my butt along the ground some more. If I stand, he'll be able to tackle me easier.

I eye his feet—they're the closest body part to me. The toes of his boots look sturdy, so I whack the mangled pipe against his ankle instead. I jump up into an immediate sprint, but the hit to his ankle doesn't even faze him. He grabs me from behind and seals me to his chest, lifting my feet off the ground. I expect a hard blow to the back of my skull to knock me unconscious, as promised.

Instead, I hear a soft whirring noise overhead. It gets louder as a gust of hot wind blows around my legs and ankles and the ground trembles. The Leaning Tower of Michelins topples over.

The Salvager shoves up my sleeve, and something hot and sharp pierces the soft underside of my forearm. I cry out but he only shoves me away from him, my skin burning. I land on all fours, but jump up again, twisting around in time to see a black-suited and helmeted Volkranian rushing toward the Salvager.

It's Ash, and she's just unsheathed a blade.

CHAPTER FIVE

THE CURVED edge of the sword winks with blue and white light. It's the same kind of sword Ash gave me months before, the one I'd hidden under the futon mattress.

The Salvager pulls something from the inside of his leather jacket—it looks like a baton, but with a flick of his wrist, it extends, and when Ash's sword comes down, the Salvager blocks it with the now long baton. He throws off the force of the sword and strikes Ash in the gut with the baton. She stumbles but doesn't fall.

I have no idea what's happening, or why it's happening, but I can't move. Can't tear my eyes away even though I should be running and checking my arm, where a burning sting feels like it's peeling away layers of my skin.

Ash's sword is a blur of motion, as is the Salvager's baton. I try to follow each blow, each block, but I have to blink—and when I do, it ends.

Ash's sword sinks into the curve between the Salvager's neck and shoulder, and he goes limp. His knees hit the dirt and when Ash extracts her sword, he falls face forward.

I stare, open mouthed, my arm on fire as Ash reaches for the chin of her helmet and rips the oblong thing off. Her white-streaked dark hair is a mess, her face still covered in black soot from earlier at the school.

"How—" I start to say, but my throat is as dry as a piece of driftwood. I don't know how she found me or how she even knew I needed help, but I'm guessing those monitors she'd mentioned observing me over the last seven months have something to do with it.

"What did he say to you?" Ash asks.

I back up, and my ankles crash into a pile of brick. I almost go down, but Ash moves forward to steady me. She grasps my burning arm and I groan before wrenching free.

"He wanted to take me somewhere. Something about a prince who would come for me... I have no idea!" I stare at the motionless body on the ground. "He's a Salvager."

Ash grimaces. "He is not a Salvager."

My forearm throbs and the muscles inside clench. I gasp and hold my arm closer to my stomach.

"You're in pain. He injured you." Ash moves forward again. "I will take you to the cityship—"

"No!" I back up. "No, I'm fine. I just twisted my arm or something."

It's a total lie—Goggles *had* done something to my arm—but I can't go to the cityship. Sam is in the garage, unconscious. The Salvager, or whatever he'd been, had said Sam would be fine, but I still need to get back to him to make sure.

"I have to go," I say, backing away.

"Penelope—"

"Here." I dig into my jeans pocket, my arm screaming in protest, and pull out the golden disc. The metal is warm, and it fits between my thumb and forefinger perfectly. Ash opens her palm, and I drop it in.

There. It's done.

"Did this have to do with the disc?" I ask.

Ash shakes her head. "Not entirely."

I don't know what that means. Another pulse of simmering pain explodes through my arm. Had he *stabbed* me? I don't feel or see any blood.

"I have to get back to Sam," I say, and then, "Thank you."

Ash stays where she is as I stumble away, clutching my arm, toward the back alley and garage.

"The sword, Penelope," she calls.

Right. Some teens hide marijuana under their mattresses. I hide an alien sword under mine.

"Not right now," I call back. "I'll...leave it out here and you can come and get it later!"

She doesn't follow me through the junkyard entrance and back into the alley, so I assume that's what she'll do. The rear door to the garage is closed, but I hear the sound of metal hammering metal.

I open the door and find Sam's back turned to me. He's hunched over the front end of the Chevrolet, just as I'd found him earlier when I'd arrived with my mom.

He straightens up and turns to me. "Hey." His eyebrows furrow. "What were you doing out there?"

I inch inside, let go of my aching arm, and look around. The groove in the pile of kitty litter where I'd scooped up a handful is still there. The dropped wrench is, too.

"Um..." The Salvager had sprayed something into Sam's face. Had it erased his memory? "I was just...bringing the trash out," I finish lamely. "How are you? Are you feeling okay?"

He *looks* okay.

Sam bends to grab a bottle of motor oil. He frowns at me as he twists off the cap. "Yeah," he says. "Why? Are you?"

I nod quickly. Telling him about the Salvager would only

complicate things. What would I say anyway? Maybe it's better if he doesn't remember anything.

And maybe that means Sam also doesn't remember trying to kiss me.

"I think I'll just...head upstairs." I hurry for the stairwell.

"I meant what I said earlier," Sam says before I can get to the bottom step. I stop and turn and see him looking at me in earnest. "I can't get out. But you, your mom, and Hayden come first."

I nod. He'd said those things before the kiss. So, he does remember at least part of our conversation. My chest tightens as he continues to stare at me.

"Tell them I'll be up in a bit," he says, then turns back to the car's engine.

I flex my fingers as I climb the stairs to the apartment. My arm isn't burning any longer, and I can't feel any blood. As I come into the kitchen and kick off my boots, voices drift from the bathroom. Hayden and my mom. The water is on, and it sounds like my mom is filling the bathtub.

Wasting no time, I go straight into the pantry and close the door. I pull the chain on the bare light bulb overhead. Light floods the small space, and I shove up my sleeve. The skin is bright pink and splotchy. There's a long, horizontal scab across my forearm. Less than an inch in length. Deep under my skin, a rectangular device shimmers, pulsing blue and purple.

Nausea churns my stomach and a cold sweat attacks my lower neck and chest. What the ever-living *hell*? I prod the skin covering the device and wince. The skin feels bruised. There's something in me, some kind of microchip.

He's not a Salvager.

I should have asked Ash *what* he was. I wish I hadn't run away so quickly, worried about Sam. He was perfectly fine, after all. I touch the skin again and flex my fingers. *What is this?* The burning is now completely gone, and all I feel is sick to my stomach.

If not a Salvager or a Volkranian—what had he been? And what had he implanted in my arm?

———

THE NEXT DAY, SCHOOLS ARE CANCELED. NOT JUST ALTON High, but the middle schools, all the elementary schools, and the local community college. Everyone knows the Salvagers had been targeting the visiting Volkranians, but they cancel school as a precaution anyway. Maybe it's just to give parents, teachers, and students a day to breathe after the bomb. Maybe it's because the Salvagers have yet to be identified and people are worried that they're loose cannons, ready to attack anyone or any institution that's pro-Peaceful Settlement—which is pretty much every institution.

My mom goes to work as usual, while Sam spends the day in the garage working on the Chevrolet again. I spend it with Hayden in the apartment, watching cartoons, feeding her endless snacks, and staring at the alien device under my skin.

I'd successfully hidden it from my mom and Sam with long sleeves the night before, but with just Hayden hanging around with her stuffed toys and Barbies, I have ample time to check the thing out a little closer.

It looks like a computer chip, with a crisscrossing network of shimmery blue and purple lines. The chip itself is about a half-inch wide and an inch long. The horizontal scab on my inner forearm must have been the insertion point. Whatever tool the Salvager used to inject the chip, it had cut shallow to avoid deeper injury, and had sealed the wound at the same time.

He hadn't been a human, I'm certain of that. He's tagged me somehow. Is it another GPS tracker? Or is it something more dangerous? I should have told Ash about it when I had the chance. The Salvager's comment about seeking an audience with the lost prince keeps nagging at me, too.

Two days after the attack, school's back in session. In astronomy class, I lose track of what the substitute teacher is saying, thinking instead about everything that had happened in the junkyard. Our regular teacher, Miss Harris, had received a laceration on her cheek from the explosion and wanted another few days to recover. I stare out the window into the courtyard and rub my arm through my long-sleeve shirt. It doesn't hurt anymore. There's a hardness just underneath my skin, but it doesn't feel bruised now.

This is ridiculous. I can't hide my arm forever. Maybe I should just show my mom and ask her to operate. She could scan it at the hospital, and then removing it would at least be sanitary. But telling her what had happened would also give her one more thing to worry about.

I'm still staring out the window, the sky a misty bank of spring storm clouds, when someone flicks off the overhead lights. Without any real sunlight outside, the room plunges into darkness. I turn away from the window and find the substitute standing in front of us, frozen. No one is near the light switch. A murmur rises from the rest of the class, and a boy named Eli, sitting closest to the classroom door, gets up to peer into the hallway.

"All the lights out there are off, too," he says.

There's a loud shuffling noise as everyone digs into bags and pockets to extract their cell phones. I'm slower than the others, but I take mine out.

"It's not working."

"Mine's not even turning on."

"Neither is mine."

I check my phone. The face is black and empty. Underneath the voices and panic starting to unfurl in room 229, there's the unmistakable silence of a power outage.

"Oh my god," Natalie Shipman, who's sitting right in front of me, says, her voice a high whine. "It's happening again. Another EMP."

"We don't know that," I tell her, but she's already fanning herself with both hands, and everyone else is getting up out of their seats.

I put my phone back in my bag and look out the window again, at the steel gray clouds hanging low. The cityship is behind the school and out of view right now, but it hangs low enough to still be seen from other windows, even with all these clouds. I'm sure the people in the classrooms with a view are crowding around their windows, looking for any signal that something is wrong.

"Settle down and get into your seats," the substitute says. No one listens.

The next few minutes are pure pandemonium. People shout and cry, and Natalie starts blowing into a paper bag that someone has scrounged up for her. I sit at my desk and keep quiet, thinking. If it's an EMP...why? The Volkranians want peace. This isn't the way to get it. But the day before yesterday, Ash had sought me out. After seven months of me having that golden disc, all of the sudden it was going to make me a target. Because something was about to happen? Something Ash and the other Volkranians knew about?

Or maybe this power outage doesn't have anything to do with the aliens. Maybe it's a Salvagers' attack, one without explosives.

The classroom door swings open and Mr. Barry, my science teacher from sophomore year, rushes in. He's breathless and pink in the cheeks.

"The school has entered a lockdown—"

A roar of voices and reactions interrupts him.

"—and you will all obey the rules of a lockdown!" he shouts above the clamor. "Until we have more information to share, you will remain in this classroom. No exceptions."

Natalie's brown paper bag flattens and expands more rapidly. I fight the temptation to pop it with my pencil.

"What if we have to go the bathroom?" Eli asks.

Mr. Barry rolls his eyes. "Do you *need* to use the restroom?"

"I might have to eventually," he replies.

A chorus of support for this protest threatens to get out of control. Mr. Barry tells our substitute good luck, and then rushes off again, most likely to relay his message down the hallway to other classrooms. I feel bad for our sub. She stands at the front of the class, eyeing the clock on the wall; the hands have stopped moving. Meanwhile, people mill around, out of their seats. Four are currently checking on Natalie. I grab my backpack—I'd found it right in my locker where I'd left it the day of the bombing—and stand up.

The only person I can think about right now is Sam. He's in Honors English two halls away. If this power outage has anything to do with the Salvagers, I want to know, and I also want to know what the point of it is.

"Excuse me," I say to our sub. Natalie might be a pain in the ass, but she's also a good excuse. "I think Natalie needs to see the nurse."

Natalie perks up in her seat, the paper bag falling away from her face as she stares at me. She nods and turns to our sub, who is probably wishing she had never said yes to covering Miss Harris's class today.

"I can take her." I grab Natalie's arm and tug so she'll stand. We're not friends, and I'm sure she's wondering why I'm suddenly so concerned, but I need out of this classroom and she's my best option.

"Okay, I suppose that's acceptable..." the substitute says, but I can hear the *I really don't give a troll's rump* underneath it. If she knew what a lockdown really consisted of, she would know bathroom runs and nurse office trips are a no-no.

I move Natalie forward toward the door, her lips once again sealed to the paper bag.

"Come right back," the sub calls as I shut the door behind us.

I direct Natalie to the right, in the direction of the nurse's office. Sam's English class is in the opposite direction, but I have to dump Natalie before heading there.

"Uh, thanks, Pen," she says as we walk through the hallway, empty except for a few teachers. One stops us, but I point to Natalie and say "nurse" and get a reluctant nod of approval.

"No problem," I tell her.

"Do you think it's the Volkranians?" she asks.

"It could be nothing."

"But our phones aren't turning on—"

"Breathe into your paper bag." For some reason her voice is burrowing into my skull, and I need it to stop. I'm not usually so impatient, which makes me think that my own panic isn't buried deep enough.

We reach the nurse's office, already packed with other kids in similar stages of anxiety attacks.

"You'll be okay? I have to go to the bathroom," I say. Natalie nods and says thank you, but I barely acknowledge it.

The door to Sam's classroom is closed, just like every other door in every hallway. *Lockdown procedure.* The top half of his door is a window, but the shade is drawn. *Lockdown procedure.*

Thankfully, I don't have to knock on the door and make some lame excuse about why.

"Pen?" Sam's forceful whisper barrels up against my back. I

spin around and find him running toward me, his bag on his shoulder. "I was on my way to get you. Come on."

He takes my hand and starts walking fast away from his classroom, toward the Vo-Tech wing where all the automotive, woodworking, and apprentice-type classes are held. Most of his classes are there, so he must know the area well. I, on the other hand, don't.

"Why are we going this way?"

He steers us down another hall, and I can smell something familiar: oil and grease and metal.

"The shop bay," he says, checking over his shoulder. "There isn't a class this block."

"Does this lockdown have to do with the Salvagers?"

He pushes open a pair of swinging doors and rushes us into a cold garage. It's silent, thankfully. A few cars are up on lifts, and in this low light, they look like those long-legged, all terrain armored transports from *Star Wars*, the kind that crash down onto their chins when their legs get tangled.

"What? No," Sam answers. He sounds annoyed, not guilty or secretive, which makes me believe him.

"Where are we going?" I ask as we move across the garage, toward the back corner where all the toolboxes are.

"I have to get to Hayden's school," he says, reaching for a door. He jiggles the knob but it doesn't move.

"Every exterior door is locked," I remind him. "That's kind of the point of a lockdown."

He holds up a finger, telling me to wait, then moves quickly toward a square piece of metal with a handle set into the wall. Sam grabs it and lifts. The metal slides up and a damp gust of wind ruffles our clothes.

"Trash hatch," he says. "There's no handle on the outside though, so once we're out, we're out. You can stay here if you want—"

A searing burn races over my forearm, nearly bringing me to my knees. I gasp and clamp my hand over the device embedded in my skin.

"Pen?" Sam lets go of the trash hatch and takes my shoulders.

"I'm coming," I say, eyes pinched shut against the pain. It feels just like it had when the Salvager had implanted it.

"What's wrong?" he asks, and seeing me clutching my arm, takes my sleeve and pushes it up. The blue and purple chip is firing off a crazy lightshow. "What the—"

I pull my arm back to my side. "I'll explain later. I have to get to my mom, though, and get this thing out of me."

It's the only option. I don't know what's happening or why the chip has suddenly flared to life, but it's starting to exhume my barely buried panic. What if it's releasing some kind of toxin into my system? Is that why it hurts?

"How did you get that thing in your arm?" he asks as I stick my leg through the open trash hatch. It comes down on the other side into a low dumpster filled with recyclables. My foot kicks through chocolate milk bottles and soda cans as I wiggle through the small square opening and breathe in the pre-rain air. It smells like pavement and grass and chlorinated pool water.

"It's complicated," I say as he ducks through the opening and joins me in the dumpster.

I clamber over the edge, my arm still throbbing.

"Who did it?" he persists.

I head out across the back parking lot of the school, toward the soccer and football fields. There's still a scorched area of grass from where the transport had been blown up.

"A Salvager," I finally answer. Sam stops me with a hand to my elbow and whips me around.

"*A Salvager?*"

"He wasn't really a Salvager though," I reply, and when he lets go of my arm, I start again into the field. There's no way off the high school grounds without being spotted from classroom windows, but there's a bike path up ahead that will get us out of sight faster than anything else.

Sam keeps my pace across the grass. "Then what was he?"

"I think he was an alien."

There. I've said it. I break into a run, as though moving faster will keep Sam's questions away.

"A Volkranian did this to you?"

The first drops of rain strike my forehead and nose.

"I don't think it was a Volkranian either." I know I'm not making any sense and I also don't know how to change that.

"Pen, when the hell did you get—?"

Sam shuts up mid-sentence, triggering an alarm bell in my head. I turn to look at him, but his attention isn't on me. I follow his stare and spot three guys walking across the soccer field. They're coming toward us.

"Do you know them?" I ask Sam.

They're tall and muscled, and they're wearing strange clothes. Gray and white tunics and black pants of some kind. Their boots are high, to the shins, and laced up. All three have some kind of Bluetooth-looking headset on. They take long, decisive strides right toward us.

"No," Sam answers.

This isn't good.

"Come on." I forget my burning forearm and grab Sam's hand. We move toward the bike path, running once again. All three men break into sprints too. A strange and familiar rippling in the air behind them catches my attention before I can face forward again. It looks like heat rising off a street in the middle of summer.

A cloaked transport?

I run faster. Sam's hand in mine is awkward, so I let go as we approach the entrance to the bike path.

But then a familiar whir above us slows me down again. Humid wind pushes into me, whipping my hair into a frenzy. I swivel as I'm running and look into the sky. One second, there's nothing but the low bank of storm clouds. The next, an alien craft is shedding its cloaking mechanism and lowering onto the field.

It's not a transport. The craft is small, like a fighter jet, and shaped like a hawk's beak. Its long nose curves down into a razor-sharp point, and the back of the craft, while shorter, is still pointed. I can't imagine how it will land on the ground and not topple over onto its side, but it manages. The craft balances perfectly on the grass. The top of the craft opens like a fighter jet too.

"Pen! Come on!" Sam shouts from the head of the bike path.

I ignore him and stare at a black-suited and helmeted Volkranian climbing from the cockpit, his hand closed around a long staff sparking blue and white veins of electricity at each spiked end.

It's the junkyard scene again, but this Volkranian isn't Ash. It's a male. So, does that mean the three, oddly dressed guys are the same things the Salvager had been? Two of them turn to meet the Volkranian head on.

He swings the staff, aiming for one of their heads. They both have the same kind of extendable baton the Salvager used, and the first one blocks the electric staff. The Volkranian is undaunted. He twirls and lunges with the sparking staff like he's a color guard on speed, and almost immediately takes out one of them by burying the spikes in his neck.

"Pen!" Sam's voice blares through my ears—he's right behind me. And that's when I notice how close the third mysterious guy has gotten to me. I've been so focused on the Volkranian that I'd lost sight of him.

Sam rushes him. The guy holds up his hand, palm out—and a sonic blast throws Sam backward, off his feet. He lands hard on the grass with a moan of pain.

Okay then. No more doubt.

These guys are definitely aliens.

"Sam—" I reach for him, but the alien grabs my arm.

I struggle, kicking my feet at his shins and punching at his chest. He holds on, the sleeve of his tunic rising just enough for me to see his own forearm shimmering with the same blue and purple under his skin. It momentarily stuns me, and I look into his eyes. They're like a multicolored marble, all green, blue, and silver swirls, centered with a constricted black pupil. Goggles hadn't had these obvious alien eyes, but he could have been wearing contacts, I suppose.

Warmth prickles along my skin. Every inch of me tingles, from my scalp to my toes, followed by a tide of lightheadedness. And then the alien holding onto me starts to dissolve. He starts to freaking *disappear*.

I open my mouth to scream, and the hiss of a laser fills the air. I know that sound, from my earlier run-ins with Volkranians —it's a lambent emulsifier. The alien arches his back, his nearly invisible face contorting with pain. He releases my arm, and as I fall backward, I catch sight of the Volkranian, ten yards away, his weapon still raised and aimed.

I land on the grass and thump the back of my head. The alien the Volkranian had been fighting strikes him across the helmet with the baton, and his reflective shield shatters. The baton then comes down onto the lambent, and it whirls out of the Volkranian's hand.

"Pen—" Sam gags for air as he crawls toward me.

The world spins and tilts from where I lay, sprawled on the

grass. The warmth and prickling of my skin are gone. When I lift my head, the alien is gone, too. The Volkranian had shot him, but it still looked as if he'd been beamed up, *Star Trek*-style.

I turn back to see the Volkranian; he's lost his lambent but still has the staff. He pivots and swings, connecting with the alien's baton. The other alien is nimble and skilled, but this Volkranian is relentless. He batters his opponent with the electric staff, beating the other alien back. He swings once more, and the spikes connect with the side of the alien's head. He topples over, twitching as electricity clambers over his body.

The Volkranian pulls off his helmet and tosses it onto the grass.

My heart thunders to a stop.

I stare, unable to breathe. Sam's voice is far away, shouting for me to get up and get moving, but I can't. I can't move. I can't understand. It's not just some Volkranian.

It's Rowan.

CHAPTER SIX

ROWAN FACES ME, his eyes dark and intense, his chest heaving for air.

"Pen, let's *go!*" Sam jerks me to my feet, but I'm limp, my body numbed by shock.

Rowan is here. *How is he here?*

I roll my shoulder and wrench my arm from Sam's grasp, stumbling forward.

"Rowan," I whisper, my voice unnaturally loud in my ears.

He stalks toward me, his electric staff lowered. With every step, he increases his speed, and I throw off Sam's hand a second and third time as I move forward to meet him.

"Stop, Pen!" he shouts. "What the hell are you doing?"

I'm doing what I've wanted to do for months. I have no idea how, but Rowan is here, and I can't run away. There's no reason to. He won't hurt me, though the ferocity in his unwavering stare the closer he gets, and the blood streaking his face from a gash on his forehead, could easily make Sam believe otherwise.

Rowan reaches for my arm as soon as he's close enough.

Sam hauls me backward. "Don't touch her!"

I throw off his hand once again. "Stop, Sam, it's okay."

Rowan stares down at Sam, his eyes narrowed with unmistakable contempt. It's the way the warden always stared at me. Only the warden's silvery eyes had never sparked with impatience or anger the way Rowan's do right now. The lines of vivid purplish blood flowing down his temple and over his eyebrow only exacerbate the threat.

He dismisses Sam without a word and reaches for my arm again. He pushes up my sleeve, gently but firmly angling my arm so he can see the shimmering device under my skin. Rowan lets out a breath and mutters a curse.

"What is it?" I ask, my eyes still roving his face, my mind still racing to keep up with what's happening.

He tugs down my sleeve, the green and blue swirls of his irises still consumed by flickering sparks. God, I've missed them.

"It is a dematerializing mechanism," he answers. His voice pulses through my ears, and I want to sob from just the sound of it. I shake my head, determined not to.

"What...what does that mean?"

"I will explain later," Rowan says, his hand still closed around my wrist. "We need to remove it."

I nod quickly. I want it out, and if Rowan knows a way to do that, I'm onboard. Sam, however, is still hovering behind me, his hands clasping my shoulders.

"What the hell is going on?" he asks again.

"Penelope is coming with me," Rowan says, though he doesn't bother to look at Sam when speaking. He doesn't look at me, either.

"Like hell she is." Sam's fingers dig into my shoulders and his mouth comes to my ear. "How does it know your name?"

It? I spin around to face him, but Rowan cuts off my retort.

"There is no time to explain. Inform Penelope's mother that I will return her once it is safe to do so."

The stiff cadence of his voice, the proper words...I've missed them, too.

Rowan starts for his aircraft, his hand still closed around my wrist. He easily pulls me from Sam's grasp. Sam runs ahead of us, half walking, half stumbling.

"Where are you going?" he shouts, nearly tripping over his own ankles.

"Please, Sam, it's okay—" I try to say again, but he won't let me.

"It's not okay! He's a Volkranian!" Sam's heel strikes the lambent emulsifier Rowan dropped earlier and he stoops to pick it up. The next thing I know, he's aiming the weapon at Rowan.

"Sam!"

Rowan stops and tugs me behind him, the arm still holding his electric staff tensing.

"Sam, stop! Put it down. Rowan—" I grasp his arm. "Don't hurt him. He doesn't know. I never told him. I never told anyone."

Sam's eyes flick between me and Rowan, and his confusion, hurt, and anger stabs me like a dull blade.

"I'm sorry," I say past a lump in my throat. "Tell my mom I've gone with Rowan and that I'll be all right. Please. She'll explain. Just...put that thing down."

He keeps it level with Rowan for another few moments. I glance toward the school for the first time. Every window facing the field is crammed with people. A bunch of students have somehow gotten outside, escaping the lockdown. A few teachers are making their way cautiously across the field toward us.

"Sam, he won't hurt me," I plead, tugging Rowan's arm. I need to get him out of here and to get this device, whatever the heck it is, out of my arm.

Sam lowers the lambent, but he doesn't hand it over. Rowan doesn't ask for it either. He keeps his body between me and

Sam, urging me forward, toward the sharp, sleek, talon-like aircraft. Heat radiates from the craft as we approach, and a soft wind pushes out against my knees and shins. The grass ripples, and I figure a kind of jet system is keeping it upright and hovering inches from the ground.

Rowan tosses his electric staff in through the top hatch and then his hands close around my waist. His touch is like a light clicking on inside a dark room. He lifts me easily, planting my butt on the rim of the hatch.

The exterior of the craft is a combination of a smooth and pearly material, like milk glass or opalescent plastic, and clear glass. I glance into the hatch, at a single, low-slung seat facing a complicated-looking panel of controls. Rowan climbs up next to me with a single hop and lowers himself into the craft. Once seated, he raises his hand to me. I don't hesitate. I swing my legs down into the hatch and take his hand. He settles me onto the seat, between his long legs. A buckle snakes out and seals us into place.

"Can you fly like this?" I ask as his arms come around me and grip a small, half-moon shaped joystick, while his fingers punch a sequence of buttons and twist several knobs in different directions. "I'm in your way."

"You are not a burden," he replies as the craft begins to hum. And then we lift from the ground in one fluid and fast motion. The force of it pushes me back into Rowan's chest. I have nothing to hold on to, so I tuck myself up into a ball, trying not to get in his way as we pierce the storm clouds.

"Relax, Penelope. You're safe," he whispers. I realize my hands are covering my face, my eyes peering out from between my fingers. I lower them slowly as the aircraft levels off. We're still lost in thick cloud cover, but Rowan doesn't seem to be nervous about it.

Rowan.

I twist around in the seat as far as the cinched lap belt will allow. He hasn't stopped glowering, and his attention is on the sky outside.

"I don't understand. How are you here?" I ask. "What just happened down there?"

His eyes don't meet mine. His jaw stays taut, his lips hardly moving when he says, once again, "I will explain later."

Monitors. We're probably being monitored the same way we had been in the transports months ago.

I face forward, cradled by Rowan's thighs and his stomach and chest, and try to steady my breathing. But when another shot of burning pain burrows into my forearm, I let out a gasp and clutch at my arm.

Rowan's stomach hardens against my back, and his hands re-grip the control wheel. The aircraft lurches, flying faster and higher into the air. We clear the clouds, and I realize just how fast and high we are.

The egg-shaped cityship is right in front of us. I can see details in the strange, pink-and-white marble exterior that I haven't before. The swirling striations glitter and move like hundreds of small rivers flowing in different directions. I want to care and wonder what the purpose for the veins of liquid are, but the burning sensation in my arm is getting worse.

"Why did they put this in me?" I ask.

"To be able to locate you," Rowan answers as he guides the aircraft toward a horizontal slit in the cityship. A cargo bay, like on the original Volkron Six, I'm betting. "And to be able to extract you from Earth."

Extract me. The other alien had started to dematerialize on the soccer field. I'd felt my own body prickling with a change I couldn't understand. I was seriously in the middle of being beamed up, too?

I twist around again, wanting to see him. *Needing* to see him. "Who were they?"

He still doesn't meet my eyes but concentrates on entering the cargo bay, holding himself rigid as we glide in. It's similar to the bay on Volkron Six, with the same white and orange uniformed cargo workers—artificers—scurrying around the vast and cavernous space.

"Inoori," he replies.

I ignore the fact that he won't look at me and think back to the last time he'd mentioned the Inoori. The warden had as well.

"The people who invaded your old planet?"

Rowan doesn't nod. He doesn't speak. And he still won't acknowledge me with a single glance. I don't get it. Is he *angry*?

He brings the aircraft to a full stop, and after a series of clanking, suctioning, and hissing noises, the hatch springs open. The belt sealing us together unlatches, retracting into the seat. I scrunch forward, snug against the control panel, and Rowan pulls himself up.

I crane my neck to see him. "If they took Volkron from you, what are they doing here?"

He lowers his hand and I take it, though hesitantly. He isn't acting the way he had back in October, and with every passing second, the ballooning sensation in my chest and stomach is starting to deflate. Rowan helps me stand, sliding me out of the craft and down onto the cargo bay floor before leaping down himself.

"I will explain later, Penelope," he says with a touch of exasperation. I clench my jaw. I'd forgotten just how infuriating and strict Rowan was in front of other Volkranians. That must be what this is. I hope.

The artificers stare at me with less wonder than they had

before, and I can only assume that's because they've grown used to the humans living below them on the ground. There have been human dignitaries who've visited the cityship a number of times too. Important people, though. Not everyday citizens like me.

Rowan proceeds through the crowd, and I follow at a close distance. We reach an elevator, and it's like the pneumatic module on Volkron Six. When we enter, the doors seal shut, and the pod is sucked up and away with the same knee-bending force. Rowan grips my elbow to help keep me from crumpling to the floor.

As soon as I can stand on my own, I whip my arm from his grasp.

"Are you going to tell me anything? Like why you're here when you were supposed to have been sent out onto the Band seven months ago?" I hold up my arm. "Like why the hell those Inoori creeps stuck this thing in my arm and wanted to *extract* me from Earth?"

His chest expands, his eyes finally meeting mine. "Volkron Six was not sent back onto the Band."

The Band is kind of like an intergalactic highway, and it's the route the Volkranians traveled to get to Earth.

"You mean you've been here...?" A hard lump forms in my throat. Like an idiot, I manage to choke out, "You've been here this whole time?"

The module jerks to the side and we come to a stop a second later, before he has the chance to answer. Or maybe he wouldn't have answered anyway.

The doors slide open, and I jump—a crowd of Volkranians greets us in a large, laboratory-looking room. There are beds and tables and monitors, and everything is white and metallic and clean. The air smells like antiseptic. I'm in a freaking alien hospital. Only to them, *I'm* the alien.

Ash comes forward as Rowan exits the module, my feet shuffling like bricks behind him.

"Commandant, I apologize. I was not aware Inoori technology had been implanted into her." Ash cuts her eyes to me and adds, "You should have told me."

Heat zings my cheeks, and I want nothing more than to lash out at her with a wise-ass retort. But I'm not angry at Ash. I yank my arm from Rowan's grasp and rub at my burning forearm.

A team of white-clad Volkranians, their heads all closely shorn and covered with caps, approaches me.

"Go with the healers," Rowan says. "They are going to remove the device."

One healer gestures toward a bed, which is raised high and surrounded by strange machines with wires, tubes, bright lights, and holographic screens hanging freely in the air. I walk away from Rowan, the lump in the center of my throat still aching.

He's acting as cold and uncaring as the warden. Indifferent. He hasn't been gone. He's been right here and he—

God, I've been so *stupid*. My teeth pinch the inside of my bottom lip to keep my chin from quivering. All these months, I'd thought he was gone. I'd thought...I'd thought I'd lost something important, and that Rowan had lost me, and that he might be enduring the same hollowed out sensation that I was.

Feeling like I've been slapped across the cheek, I follow the healers to the high table. The cushion underneath molds to my form as I'm positioned onto my back.

Ash and Rowan are still speaking in low voices near the pneumatic module, neither one of them glancing my way. Their conversation is intense and heated, but they each snap to silent attention when the module doors glide open again. A female emerges.

I take in her black hair and blunt bangs. It's the female Volkranian I'd met in October, in the Manhattan building where the previous Fleet Commandant had set up a Volkranian base. Pencil Skirt, I'd dubbed her. Only, she's not wearing human clothes as she had been then. She's in a black, full body uniform like all the Volkranian males. Hers, however, hugs her curves.

She stabs me with a glare—just as she had months back—before moving to Rowan's side. One of the white-robed Volkranian healers chooses that moment to block my view. He pushes my sleeve to my elbow and inserts my arm into a clear tube that one of the other healers has just swung into place. A circular wall closes around my elbow, sealing my arm inside. Another closes around my wrist, leaving my hand sticking out the other end.

A gentle hand rests on my shoulder and presses, as if to hold me in place. A laser flash inside the tube is followed by a hot prickling on my skin. The scabbed-over, inch-long wound where the device had been injected has been reopened. My stomach churns as blood trickles from the wound. A track laid into the top of the tube zips into action, guiding a long, thin metal arm and a pair of fine-tipped pincers to just above the opening. The metal arm extends and the pincers peel back my skin.

"Oh my god." I squeeze my eyes shut so I don't have to watch.

A cold sweat breaks out on my chest and the back of my neck as the pressure of the pincers digs inside my arm. It doesn't hurt, though. I take deep breaths and wait for some burst of pain, but it doesn't happen.

My fingers clench and release on the other end of the tube, my palm clammy, and then the unsettling pressure is gone. A hurricane-grade blast of air blows around inside the tube, and I open my eyes as another laser flash brightens the tube. It prickles, like a bug bite, and then the circular walls holding my wrist and elbow release. The tube is swung away, my arm coming free, as Ash approaches the bed.

A healer shakes his head at Ash and says something in Volkranian. She frowns. I notice the pincers inside the tube are empty. My arm starts to throb again, and a glance at my newly healed wound shows colorful lights dancing underneath my skin.

"It's still in there," I say, my stomach churning yet again.

I push up onto my elbows, my head spinning. I want it *out*.

"The Inoori device has already reacted with your biology," the healer says, in English this time, but my ears are ringing with panic. I close my eyes and try to listen. "We cannot remove it without severely damaging the nerves and muscles of your forearm. And attempting to disable it with an electromagnetic pulse could have unintentional complications."

I open my eyes and gape at him. "What do you mean? It's in there forever?"

Ash comes forward. "Leaving it in won't harm you. Taking it out will. For now, it's best to leave it as it is."

I can't speak. There's an alien device stuck in my arm that might make my body dematerialize at any second. And it won't *harm* me?

My attention jumps from the lights under my skin to Rowan and Pencil Skirt hashing something out in the back corner of the room. Rowan has a cloth and is wiping the blood from his face, a healer hovering nearby with a tray of supplies, her eyes on the angled gash just above his eyebrow.

"It is old Inoori technology," Ash goes on. "The one I fought the other day in your presence had lived aboard Volkron Six for twenty years. He must have had this among his possessions since leaving Volkron."

"Great, so I have expired alien tech in my body," I mutter as

I swing my legs over the side of the bed. "But why would a Volkranian have Inoori technology?"

Ash lowers her voice. "He was not Volkranian. He was an Inoori spy."

A spy. He'd hidden among them in plain sight for two decades. "But...the Inoori took your planet. They won the war, right? Why would they send a spy with the Volkranians who were fleeing?"

It doesn't make sense.

Ash glances over her shoulder. Rowan and Pencil Skirt are still discussing something, and the healer is now applying something to his forehead. Pencil Skirt's nostrils flare in anger, her eyebrows pinched. Rowan's expression is of barely contained fury. Something stirs to life in the lowest part of my stomach as I watch them interact. Something I don't want to acknowledge.

"I would not have known he was Inoori," Ash says, turning back to me. "But then you mentioned something about a prince."

A prince. Right. Goggles had mentioned wanting an audience with Prince Someone-or-another.

"Do you recall the prince's name?" she asks.

Goggles had spoken so swiftly, and my adrenaline had been rushing, my mind in survival mode. I think it started with a T, but I can't be sure.

"Penelope?"

I reluctantly divide my attention from Rowan and Pencil Skirt and see Ash cross her arms.

"Sorry," I say, my tongue feeling swollen and clumsy. "I don't know."

The healer finishes with Rowan and darts away, leaving him and Pencil Skirt to continue their heated discussion. "What's her name?" I ask. "Does it have a translation?"

Ash nods. "Dove."

It's awful. It makes her sound soft and pure and beautiful. I don't know if she's the first two, but she definitely has that third one down.

Ash lowers her voice and says, "All high-ranking Volkranians are matched soon after release from the chamber."

I take a second to funnel that information into my mind and make sense of it. Released from the chamber, for Volkranians, means being born.

"Matched?"

I guess it's pretty straightforward what that means too, but I'm hoping I'm wrong. I'm hoping it means something else. Like matched with an occupation.

"With a mate," she clarifies.

I nod, my head bobbing uncontrollably. Right. A mate. Matched. Rowan and Pencil Skirt. It's obvious now. I mean, she'd hated me on the spot, sending death glares my way every chance she got. And Rowan had let me believe he was gone for seven months. He hadn't been happy to see me back on the high school soccer field. He hasn't looked my way once since coming into this operation room. Because he's matched. Does that mean *married*? Contractually bound?

I don't care. I *don't*. It doesn't matter, and I block the next images that try to come forward—the one of Rowan kissing me. Of him assuring me that humans and Volkranians are *physically compatible*. I can't even count the number of times I've gone over and over those words in my head the last several months, or how often I've felt regret over pushing him away before he could kiss me again.

My fingers tuck into my palms so hard the joints start to ache. My teeth pin the inside of my lower lip again. And that lump in my throat? It's a baseball now.

"Right," I whisper around it, sliding down off the bed and onto my feet.

What had I been thinking? I'm a human. Lowly and primitive and a joke in the eyes of the Volkranians.

I clear my throat and fling questions at Ash, so I won't have to think about the chasm opening inside my chest. "So why would that Inoori spy approach me after twenty years of hiding? Why inject me with the device? I was almost beamed up somewhere—where would I have gone?"

With a jerk of her head, Ash motions toward a strip of windows. I follow her, resisting the screaming urge to look over at Rowan and Dove again.

"You would have gone there," Ash answers, pointing with her black gloved hand out the window. I look, but all I can see is sky, dark slate and thick with rain clouds.

"The clouds?" That can't be right.

Ash doesn't say anything. She just keeps looking out the window. So, I do the same. After a handful of awkward seconds, just when I'm about to ask what the hell we're supposed to be looking at, the sky pulses with lightning. That's when I see it, there and gone again as the flickering lightning peters out.

They aren't just clouds. There is a mist, yes, hanging in the sky, but they aren't storm clouds. It's a shield of some kind. A forcefield. When the lightning flashed, I saw through it, to the dense outline of a ship; an enormous ship, larger than the original Volkron Six, larger than any of the other Volkranian city-ships across the world. Except maybe the Tokyo ship, Volkron One, which has been measured to be half the size of Manhattan.

In the brief glance the lightning had given me, I'd seen what looked like a mountain hanging in the sky. A black, steeple-topped, bowl-bottomed mountain.

"What is that?" I whisper against the glass.

"Avorra," Ash replies.

I stare into the clouds, terrified but mesmerized. "What is Avorra?"

Rowan's voice comes from behind us. "The Inoori mothership."

I ignore my instinct to swivel around and look at him. I won't make a bigger fool out of myself than I already have.

I take a breath. "Is that what sent out the EMP?"

"Yes. It exited the Band early this morning and continued on a course to Earth," Rowan replies. "As soon as it was in place here, it erected an aegis dome over the New York City area."

"What does the dome do?" I ask.

"It keeps us in, and the rest of the world out," Ash answers.

"But the EMP hasn't affected the Volkranian ships?" I ask.

"Not on the same level," is the vague answer I get from Rowan, while Ash arches an eyebrow. So they're affected, but not incapacitated like the humans.

"Those three Inoori you fought just now—" I make the mistake of turning to see Rowan. Pencil Skirt—*Dove*—is right there at his side, her arctic glare on full blast. "Did they come from that ship?"

Rowan nods once. He ignores me, his attention on the window and the ship beyond.

"What do they want?" I ask.

"There has not yet been any contact between our ships," Rowan answers, but Dove interrupts him.

"The only movement they've made is the attempt to extract you." She says that last word—*you*—with implicit meaning. She can't understand why anyone would possibly want to take me anywhere. I guess I don't really understand it, either.

"I've had that dematerialization device in me for two days. Why did they send someone to get me? Why not just beam me up right away?"

"It's old technology," Ash repeats. "They could have attempted it, but if there had been a glitch during the dispersal of your molecules, you would have died."

Holy science, Batman. My molecules had been *dispersing*, and that was considered *old* technology?

"Newer dematerialization mechanisms provide for side-by-side extraction," Ash explains. I nod, but really, I'm just thankful my molecules are all where they're supposed to be. And I guess it's a good sign that they hadn't wanted to accidentally kill me.

But my biggest question still hasn't been answered: "Why did they want to extract me in the first place? I'm a human."

"A human who has had contact with the Volkranian people in the past," Ash says. "And they were under the impression that this prince they wish to speak to would come for you."

Her eyes slide to Rowan and stick.

I blink at him. Sure, his position was similar to the human concept of royalty, but why would they want to lure Rowan to their ship? Why would they have left the planet they'd won in the first place? There's no traveling backward on the Band, I've been told. They couldn't return. Could they?

"How is your arm?" Rowan asks, his eyes touching on me for less than a heartbeat. There's no missing the obvious way he's avoiding the subject of the Inoori.

I rub the incision again, amazed at how fast it has healed. "Still filled with dangerously old Inoori technology."

He nods. "I'll see you to your room." Rowan steps aside, expecting me to fall into step.

But right then, even a steamroller couldn't have plowed me down. "My *what*?"

Dove makes a clicking noise in her throat. "Keeping her on the cityship is a mistake."

I hate that I agree with her. "I'm not staying. I can't. Besides, you told Sam that you'd bring me home."

Sam, who'd likely kick my mom and me out now that he

knew the truth: I'm not just a sympathizer. I'm a traitor. And a liar.

"I said I would bring you home when it was safe." The colors of Rowan's irises collide like a storm front. "It is not yet safe. Until it is, you will stay with me."

I'm not the only one staring at him, my lips parted in surprise. Dove looks like she's just swallowed her own tongue, and Ash steps away from the window, as if she'd like to remove herself from the conversation entirely.

There's no wiggle room. No opening for me to argue and insist that I be taken back to my house. And anyway, if those Inoori people return for another shot at me, I don't want my mom or Sam or Hayden to be anywhere in the vicinity.

"Okay," I say.

Clearly, Rowan isn't prepared for such an easy surrender. He waits another moment, eyeing me cautiously, before saying once again, "I'll show you to your room."

This time, I go.

CHAPTER SEVEN

THE PNEUMATIC MODULE takes us through a confusing system of pipeline, zooming past open spaces and corridors; cavernous rooms filled with Volkranians and machinery; atriums filled with light and trees and grass. I even get a three-second glimpse of a room filled with clear water tanks, with things like fish swimming around inside, only they're long with cotton-candy-pink scales.

I keep my attention on the spaces we pass, and Rowan and I stand in silence. I have questions. Endless questions. Why are the Inoori here? Is Rowan a Volkranian prince? Is he still fleet commandant? Where is the original Volkron Six? What's going to happen now?

I don't ask any of my questions, though not because of the monitors watching us. If I dare part my lips and speak, I know the only thing I'm going to do is make myself look like a heart-sick idiot who'd actually believed she was more important to him than she really was.

But as we travel upward, to the side, up again, then down a little through the pneumatic system, the module starts to feel warm instead of cold. Rowan's silence isn't frosty like it had been before. Listening to him now, with no interruption, I can hear his breathing is off. Every now and then he shifts his footing, restlessly.

He wants to speak. I can feel it. I assume the monitors in the module with us are stopping him, but maybe I'm wrong about that, too. Maybe I'm imagining all of it. Maybe my imagination has been playing me for a fool since October.

We come to a stop and the doors slide open. He waits for me to exit first and then quickly takes the lead. I follow, trying to keep up with his strides. He's walking fast enough as it is, so I'm left jogging in his wake. Finally, he stops in front of a metal door. It glides open and Rowan stands aside. I stare at his boots. My guestroom awaits.

I edge past him, into a small, spare room. It's not as large as his had been on Volkron Six, and it doesn't have the same sleek quality. This looks more like a walk-in closet, with a single bed attached to a wall, a desk, a slim, horizontal window, and in the corner, a door that hopefully leads to a bathroom.

My feet move across the glossy, black floor toward the window. It still looks cloudy and stormy outside, and once again, I realize I'm up high, among the Volkranians, while the other humans are trapped in confusion and fear on the ground. Another EMP. Another species entering our atmosphere. At this point, people on the ground probably haven't seen the new spacecraft. *Avorra.* An honest-to-goodness alien *mothership*.

The door seals shut behind me. I feel him still standing there. The deflated feeling in my chest and stomach had started to reverse while we'd been in the module together, even though my throat had stayed tight. I try to swallow the knob lodged there and turn to face him.

Rowan's stare slams into me. Finally, there's nothing impersonal or cold about it. It's a hot, physical push. Exactly how I've wanted him to look at me: the way he had months ago, when he'd kissed me. Rowan flexes his fingers at his sides. His chest expands with a deep, measured breath, but when he exhales, I hear it shake.

"Penelope," he whispers.

He sweeps across the snug room in two quick strides and before I can say anything, his palms are cradling my cheeks, his mouth inches away from mine.

"I'm sorry," he whispers, his lips touching mine once and retreating.

"Rowan—"

He covers my mouth with his, and this time, he doesn't pull away. The force of his kiss shoves me back a step, but he catches me, hooking my waist with his arm and pinning me against him. He has to stoop to kiss me, even though I'm on my toes, my body throbbing, my head spinning.

Rowan lifts me from the floor and positions me higher, so that I hover an inch or two over him. I keep kissing him. Keep touching his face and threading my fingers through his hair, trying not to think about the fact that he'd waited until we were alone before letting down his guard. Maybe it's just a Volkranian thing. Maybe it's more than that. I don't know anything except that I can't pull away from him.

"I'm sorry," he says again as he takes the last step toward the bed. He slides me down the front of his body, his hands still roaming and touching, my skin still leaping underneath them.

"If there had been a way for me to send word to you, to tell you where I was, I would have," he says with his lips buried in my hair at the crown of my head.

"You were here?"

"No. On the asteroid belt circling Mars."

I hike my chin and stare up at him. "Seriously?"

"It borders the entrance onto the Band." His palms run up and down my back, leaving gooseflesh in their wake. I lean into his chest, wanting only to sink into him. Not that I can really sink into any part of him. He's a wall of muscle.

"The Sovereign positioned Volkron Six there as an outpost. He didn't wish for anyone to know, though, not even the Volkranians...in case any others thought to go against his directives," he explains.

I close my eyes and try to focus on what he's telling me. The Sovereign's punishment for waging violence against the humans had just been for show? He'd lied to the world, to his own people, letting us all think he'd disciplined the ship that had disobeyed his directives. He hadn't been willing to sacrifice them, though.

"What were you doing there this whole time?" My hands slide up his chest and circle around, holding him closer.

Rowan sits onto the edge of the bed and pulls me into his lap. His thighs aren't exactly comfortable cushions, but it doesn't matter. I'd sit here all day if I could. "Monitoring the Band. Listening for signals that were preceding any approaching crafts."

"And you heard the Inoori coming," I say.

He nods, his hand lifting mine so he can kiss the tips of my fingers. He'd missed me. Every reverent touch and kiss screams it in a way no words ever could.

"Where is Volkron Six now?" I ask, my voice strangely breathy from something as simple as fingertip kisses.

"Gone," he answers, his mouth traveling to my palm, and then my inner wrist. It's an electric shock, straight to the space between my hips. "It's returning to the asteroid belt to make sure no other Inoori craft arrive."

With every press of his lips, I feel myself coming apart. The shabby wall I'd thrown up around my heart over the last few months to forget how he'd made me feel collapses like wet cardboard. I'd told myself so many times that missing him as much as I did was deranged. That I had to be romanticizing him, or that I only *thought* I missed and wanted him so badly because I *couldn't* have him. But no part of the storm firing off inside me right now feels romanticized or exaggerated or false in any way.

"Rowan."

He lowers my hand and looks at me again. His eyes are sooty green, the blue almost entirely consumed.

"Why am I here?"

His thumb brushes my lower lip. "I was telling the truth—I want you safe, and you won't be safe on the ground." He keeps his eyes on my mouth. "And because I think I have been lied to."

I cover his hand with mine, needing him to stop. "Please. I can't think when you do that."

A smile tugs at the corner of his mouth. "Not thinking sounds like something I would enjoy."

Just like the last time we'd sat on a bed together, on the first Volkron Six, when reality had been a thousand miles away. Neither of us had been thinking then, either.

I push his hand down. "Who's lied to you?"

He lets out a breath and shifts me off his lap so he can stand. A part of me regrets asking him to stop, but the other part of me can't forget the gigantic Inoori mothership hanging over New York City in unnatural cloud cover.

"The spy said the prince would come for you. I'm not a prince, but I *am* the only Volkranian who would bend to the demands of an Inoori holding you captive."

I stand up from the edge of the mattress. "What about Ash? She said she felt compelled to help me because I had been...*of interest* to you. Her words, not mine," I add.

Rowan sets his feet wider apart and cocks his head. "Ash?"

Of course. That's not what Rowan calls her. "Your friend. It's one of the translations for her name."

He nods, understanding but still frowning. "I suppose she might feel the need to protect you, but she is not a prince."

"Oh, right." *Duh, Pen.* "So, you think someone has lied, then? A Volkranian?"

Rowan nods, his eyes once again on the slim, horizontal window. "It's not so hard to imagine. I spent nearly twenty years being lied to—the whole ship did. We were trained to rid the earth of humans, when the Sovereign had given no such orders."

Yes, the original fleet commandant had lied. But why lie about Rowan being a prince? "Prince of what?" I ask. "Do Volkranians even have princes?"

He rubs his forehead, massaging the space between his eyebrows. "No." He drops his hand and turns to face me. He looks angry and ready for war. "But the Inoori do."

It takes a few moments for me to process what he's saying: The Inoori believe Rowan is an *Inoori* prince?

He walks to me, his body looming over mine as he touches my arms. He rubs them in what I'm sure he means to be a soothing and relaxing way, but he's so strong he easily tugs me against his chest and stomach. Not that I mind.

"I need to make contact with Avorra." His lips move against my head, his breath fanning over my hair and scalp. "You'll be safe in here. And I'll return as soon as I can."

Rowan's hands slip with confident ease from my arms to my hips. He pulls me closer, but as much as I want to just revel in his touch, I have more questions.

"Why wouldn't you look at me earlier? Why were you so angry with me?"

He lets out a breath, heavier than before, and his fingers slip up along my ribs. "I was not angry with you. I'm sorry if that is how it appeared."

"Then what was wrong?"

"If there was one spy on this ship, there is likely to be more.

I hoped looking indifferent to your presence would convince them that you are not the easiest way to get to me."

Rowan's lips trace my hairline, the warmth between our bodies rising to a slow boil. I need to get back on land, and home, but the idea of spending the night on the cityship with the possibility of Rowan coming back to my room and doing, well...more of this...is tempting.

"If you wanted other spies to think you didn't care, you shouldn't have demanded that I stay on this ship," I point out.

"Do you want to leave? I will send three of my guards with you for protection if so."

I shake my head. "Honestly? I don't want to leave just yet. I...I missed you."

A grin tugs at the corner of his mouth, but it doesn't form fully before concerned sadness takes over. He touches my cheek, his thumb sweeping across my bottom lip. "I longed for you every day."

He *longed* for me. For once, his formal choice of words doesn't make me want to laugh. It lights me on fire. I get up onto my toes, and Rowan must read the intention on my face because he lowers his head to meet me in the middle. I kiss him, savoring his lips and the greedy, protective scoop of his arms as he brings me closer.

I can forgive him for his initial cool distance. Especially if he thought it might persuade any potential Inoori spies to rethink their plan to use me as bait. But I need to make sure he knows that's over now.

I drop onto my heels and break from the kiss. Confusion over why knits his eyebrows.

"If I stay, even just for one night, I don't want you to treat me like that. Like I don't matter."

His eyes soften. "You have my vow."

I bite my lower lip, trying not to smile. Rowan and his vows.

So chivalrous. "Okay then, I'll stay," I say lightly. "I'm sure you're right and it's safer. I don't want my mom, Sam, or Hayden in any danger anyway."

Rowan stills. "The male on the ground, who wanted you to leave with him. That is Sam?"

I know it's immature to like the jealousy packed into his question, but I can't help it. "Yeah. He's a friend that my mom and I have been living with. His sister is Hayden."

Rowan's fingers resume caressing my lower back. "You didn't tell him what happened."

I rub my nose into his chest and breathe in his scent. That clean, midnight snow scent that I'd almost forgotten about. "I couldn't tell anyone. People who sympathize with the Volkranians have a tendency to turn up dead or missing."

Rowan pulls back and gazes down at me. "I've put you in danger."

"In more ways than one, it seems," I reply, but then smile. "I don't regret it though."

Troubled darkness crosses his expression. "If you're harmed and I'm the reason—"

I thump his chest with my palms. "You've brought me here to keep me safe. I trust you." I shrug, deciding to take a chance at bearing my soul. I'm not brave enough to look at him while I do it though. "And I care about you. A lot."

Rowan doesn't say anything, and after a moment of quiet, I glance up to see if I've made a complete fool of myself. But he's only staring at me, his expression serious.

"I hoped you had not forgotten me."

I gape at him, ready to laugh and ask how in the world that could have ever happened. But he blinks, then lets me go and steps away. His jaw is rigid, his brows pulled into a serious line over his eyes. "The door will only open for myself, the fleet commandant, and the warden—*Ash*, I mean."

I want to go with him, not stay inside this stark, small room. But I know I can't.

"What about Dove?" I ask, and remembering that's not what he calls her, add, "The other girl."

Rowan holds still by the door. There's barely a shift in his posture, but I can still see agitation in the small flare of his nostrils and the press of his lips. "She will not visit you."

"You're matched," I say, trying like hell not to let my jealousy show the way he had when asking about Sam. Rowan frowns and I admit, "Ash told me."

"Yes, we are." His answer isn't exactly heavy with remorse, but I do hear something in it. Some kind of disappointment.

"What, exactly, does being matched mean?" It's probably not the best time to get into the finer details, but I can't curb my curiosity. "Are you two...a couple or something?"

And if so, why the hell is he kissing *me*? That should have been one of the first things we talked about, but I'd been caught up in the moment, I guess.

Rowan takes a second to consider, his eyes pensive. Then says, "We are not a couple as defined by human terms. We are matched because it was determined that when paired, our genetic compositions would produce exceptional descendants."

I blink, a bit addled by the stilted words. After taking a second to translate them into plain English, I'm pretty sure I grasp his meaning. "Wait. So you two were matched because you'd make amazing babies?"

I might actually want to puke.

He takes a fortifying breath. "That is the reason why most Volkranians are matched, Penelope. It doesn't have anything to do with affection."

Closing my eyes, I try to take this in. If it's really that unemotional, why had Dove been so fierce toward me?

"But she does have feelings for you. Doesn't she?"

Rowan sighs. "Yes. And there was a time when I returned them."

Oh. Envy twists low in my stomach.

"That hasn't been the circumstance for quite some time," he adds, with a subtle lift of one dark brow and the shadow of a grin on his lips.

Oh. My stomach flutters.

"Does that mean you aren't still matched?"

Rowan frowns and makes a rare human motion, rubbing the back of his neck as if uncomfortable. "We can discuss it tonight. I'll return as soon as I can, but I do have to go."

Of course he does. Rowan approaches the door, and it opens for him on a whisper of air. What I really want is to keep him here and let everyone else deal with Avorra. I want him to assure me that he doesn't still plan to combine his and Dove's superior DNA to make the ultimate super baby.

But I know, even without the title of fleet commandant, Rowan is the Volkranian in charge, and his people need him. So, I nod and put on a brave smile. He leaves, the door sealing shut behind him.

I eye the bed. I know better than to lay down on the kidney bean-shaped pillow. The last time, I'd been taken on a trippy kind of nap, and it had left my head hazy for several minutes after. My mind had been clear when I'd kissed Rowan though, so I knew I couldn't blame that on the drugged-up pillow.

I'd felt stabs of guilt back in October for kissing him, but today, I only want him to come back into the room. I don't feel guilty. I feel *needy*. For his lips, his touch, his voice. And an explanation about Dove, good or bad. I just want answers.

Ten minutes after Rowan has left, I'm already bored. And anxious. And hungry. I wish there was a television or tablet, something to tell me what's happening either on the ground or around the cityship. In this small room, I feel like I'm tucked away from the entire world. Forced into solitary confinement for my own good. Ten minutes and already my muscles ache from restlessness, and the device implanted in my arm is still stinging in random pulses. Like someone, somewhere, is pushing a button and trying to extract me. It makes me shiver, and I close my eyes, questioning if maybe the kidney bean pillow and drifting away on a haze of drug-induced sleep isn't such a bad idea after all.

I lay down, tentatively. But a second later, a loud beeping sound has me bolting upright again. A holographic screen pops up next to the room's door, and filling it is a familiar face: a woman with shorn hair and a kind smile. She was one of the healers; the one who'd helped Rowan with his wounded forehead. I rise from the bed.

"Hello? Penelope?" Her voice has the filtered sound of someone talking into a speaker.

"Uh, hi?" I look for a button to push, like an apartment building intercom. There's nothing, but she hears me anyway.

"I am a healer from earlier. Do you recall me?"

"Yes," I reply, speaking loudly. She smiles, like she's amused, and I guess that I don't have to yell to be heard.

"I have a balm that will help numb the discomfort the device is giving you. I meant to apply it to your arm before you left the hospital chambers."

As if on cue, a stinging sensation stronger than the others burrows into my forearm. I clutch at it, hissing against the pain. I have to get this freaking thing out of me. Until then, a numbing balm sounds just about perfect.

"Hold on," I say, approaching the door. It doesn't move the way it had for Rowan. I panic for a moment, thinking maybe he hasn't granted me the ability to open the door, and that I'm trapped inside. A swell of claustrophobia barrels down my throat.

There's a wall-mounted plate near the hologram screen. I lift my hand to it. Nothing. I lower my face to look closer, and then hear the click and hiss of the door sliding open. The wall-mounted plate must have read my retina or something. On the other side of the door, the healer's hands grip a metal tray filled with white cloths, glass jars, and other medical looking things.

"Thanks," I say as she enters the room.

Moving with deliberate care and gentleness, she sets the tray on the small table next to the bed. She and the rest of the healers seem totally different than the Volkranians I've met so far. Instead of icy expressions, they wear smiles. Apparently, bedside manner isn't just a thing that humans appreciate.

I roll up my sleeve, ready for the ointment. She comes toward me, reaching for my arm.

"Just relax," she says. But she doesn't have the ointment. I look back at the tray.

"Don't you need the—"

She grabs my arm with both of her hands and digs her fingers in, tight.

"All will be well, Penelope," she says, but at that very moment, the chip in my arm explodes with pain.

CHAPTER EIGHT

I TRY TO WRENCH AWAY, but the healer is too strong.

"Stop!" I cry.

"Do not resist," she says calmly.

Bursts and pops of light fire off around me, like millions of camera flashes. Only parts of the healer's face and body are visible—she's dissolving as I try to pry her hands from my arm. But *my* hands...they're like the blinding flare of sparklers that kids run around with on the Fourth of July.

I hold up my free arm and stare at the swirling maelstrom of white, gold, and red lights. My arm is no longer solid; a tingling sensation, like an errant sip of soda fizzing up my nose, throbs everywhere. My whole body pulses. And then my feet lift from the floor.

I spiral upward, toward the ceiling, in a dizzying swirl of light. I'm pulled and stretched and spun as the coarse rub of prickling heat goes on and on. I'm dying; I must be. I'm being pulled apart and I'm never going to see Rowan again, or my mom or Sam or Hayden or Mister Mister.

But then, the brightness fades, and solid ground shoves up against my feet.

My knees bend and fold from sudden gravity. The flares of light bulbs exploding in my eyes extinguish as my hands come down hard on a metal surface. I gulp air into my lungs as my fingers, from the knuckles up, reform like sand solidifying. I stare at the tips of my fingers as they reappear before my eyes and swallow a scream.

A hand grabs my arm and hauls me up, off my knees and to my feet. The healer is with me still, but she's not the one who's holding on to me. She's still smiling, as if she hasn't just pulled a total Evil Queen move. The healer could have come knocking on my door with a basket of apples and I would have taken a bite. I'm such a *moron*.

I'm now in a room with glass walls, and behind the glass, a crowd of people stands, staring in at me. No. Not *people*. Not *humans*. My pulse is still staccato, and my vision unsteady, but two of them smirk. They hold up their hands and goggle at their fingertips, the way I just did. I can't believe it—the aliens are making fun of me! *Jerk faces.*

The one holding me gives me a rough push, and I stumble forward on wobbly knees. My heart beats wildly and my head feels light as I'm ushered from the room. I pass the two jerks that are still laughing at me. If I didn't think they might kill me, I'd flip them off.

I'm on the Inoori ship. Avorra. I'm certain of it.

Oh god. Rowan is going to be *so pissed*.

The alien hustles me toward another entranceway. I twist around to spear the healer with a hateful glare, but she's gone. My feet trip over themselves and the alien grunts and swears—in English, I notice—as he fights to keep me upright.

"Who are you?" My tongue is heavy and awkward in my mouth. I wriggle my arm and try to throw off the alien's hand. "Let go!"

His iron grip is unrelenting as he forces me through a pipe-like hallway, our feet clanging against a metal floor. My muscles are sore and tight, and the entire surface of my skin feels like it's just been exfoliated with broken glass.

"Where are you taking me?" I ask, and when we turn a corner and go another half-dozen steps in silence, I add, "I know you can understand me. Where am I?"

He still says nothing. He just stares straight ahead, keeping his profile to me. We reach the end of the tube-shaped hallway, and my eyes stick on the opening. My depth perception tells me it empties onto a balcony. There's a drop off, and across the abyss, is a solid wall of lush green foliage. Gnarled tree roots weave between clumps of hanging moss and wet leaves. A red-winged bird flaps through the air. Humidity laps my face and neck as the alien drags me around the corner and onto a gallery walk.

I stare over the thick partition and see it's only one of many that step down a multi-leveled shaft. What looks like a jungle—an actual *jungle*—is on the other side. The sweet scent of flowers and water reminds me of the time my parents took me and Ollie to Disney's Animal Kingdom.

But I'm on a spaceship.

A spaceship with a jungle.

I stop fighting the alien. There isn't a point, really, just like there hadn't been a point in fighting Rowan when he'd taken me aboard Volkron Six that first time. I don't have friends here. I can't beam myself back down to Earth or back to the egg-shaped cityship. All I can do is try to keep up with what's going on, though the jungle to my right is making that difficult.

The alien approaches an archway that fills the width of the gallery walk. It looks like a giant metal detector, though there's nothing beyond it except a wall. He walks toward it at full speed, his hand still wrenching my upper arm. The archway hums with energy, as if powering up, and without slowing down, he steps through. I inhale and tense up, certain we're going to strike the cement wall on the other side.

Instead, my vision balloons and snaps back to normal, and I'm suddenly walking into a cathedral. At least, that's what it looks like at first. No pews, though. Just open floor. I glance behind us and see a matching arch like the one we just crossed through. No jungle. No gallery walk. Just a long, empty room.

I stumble and face forward. Up ahead, an enormous, floor-to-ceiling window, cut up by panels of stained glass and fancy lead work, lets in the stormy light outside. A semi-circular set of steps leads to an altar, an ornate throne topping it. Seated on the throne, is a woman.

Her vibrant green dress is close to the color of the jungle I just passed. The air here is no longer muggy, but crisp. The alien hurries me through the colossal room, the ceiling so high I can't see anything but black when I crane my neck. When I look ahead again, the woman's eyes lock on mine. She has her hands folded together on her lap in a patient manner. She's older and pretty, though there are lines near her eyes and dark hollows at her cheekbones and temples.

Her hard and unyielding stare chills me. At the first step leading to the altar, the alien stops and drops to one knee in a fast bow. He yanks me down with him, and I end up slamming my knees onto the black floor. Pain rockets through my kneecaps.

"Queen Ursa, your order is fulfilled," he says, his hand an iron weight on my arm, holding me down beside him.

"Rise," the woman says. Her voice echoes through the room.

I'm yanked back up into a standing position, and along with my aching knees comes an unexpected tide of fury and panic. I wrench my arm and shove at the alien, but he's built like a refrigerator, and I'm sure I'm the equivalent of a kitten swiping at a mastiff.

"Let. Me. *Go*," I growl. "Where do you think I'm actually going to run off to?"

He shifts his eyes to me. They brim with annoyance.

"Release her," the queen says, her voice calm and husky. It doesn't go with her air of elegance, and it makes her sound much older than she appears.

The beefcake drops my arm. It throbs now that it's no longer constricted. *Damn.* That's going to leave a bruise.

Queen Ursa sits serenely on her throne, still inspecting me. "Welcome aboard Avorra, Penelope. I apologize for the way you were brought here, however it was a necessary discourtesy."

She stands then, her green dress swishing like silky water around her legs. The fabric glimmers and a jeweled headdress winks at me. The gems look like diamonds and rubies and amethysts. It's more extravagant than anything I've seen on Volkron Six.

I rub my arm as my eyes skip around the room. It's totally vacant, except for the dais and throne that Queen Ursa has been sitting on. "Why am I here?"

She descends the first few steps from the dais. "You are incentive."

"You mean bait," I reply.

"Precisely." The queen comes down a few more steps, hands clasped together in front of her. "You could also describe it as such. However, that word has such negative energy surrounding it. Incentive, at least, points to an opportunity at hand."

"Does that opportunity involve me getting beamed back down to the ground?"

The queen cracks a smile. "No."

"Then I'll stick to calling it *bait*."

I don't care if I'm being pushy or impertinent. Just like well-behaved women rarely make history, I'm willing to bet well-mannered humans rarely survive on enemy alien spacecrafts.

Before I can ask another question, a brief, ear-piercing chime rings out. I wince as she turns and takes tranquil steps back up to her throne. There's another sound, this time from behind me, like the hum of a microwave oven. A plasma-like ripple of blue light fills the arched portal. It snaps and fades, and another alien strides through.

I gape at him. At his brown hair, touched by gold. His hard, stony eyes, the color of jade and sky. The angular cut of his nose and cheeks, too sharp for the fullness of his mouth.

He looks like *Rowan*. But...it isn't him. He glares at me, as if I've offended him by just standing here. I hold his icy stare as he closes in on me.

"Kronan, my son," Queen Ursa says.

He's a prince, then. Cards shuffle up next to one another in my mind, trying to get in line and show me the hand I've been given. But just then, a life-size holographic screen pops up to my left, to the side of the steps leading to the dais, and the cards collapse.

The image is transparent—I can see through it, to the rest of the queen's throne room—but the figures standing before us are fully formed and even a little three dimensional: the warden, Ash, Dove, a Volkranian dude I don't know, and the only one that turns my stomach into a carnival's tilt-a-whirl ride—*Rowan*.

I move forward, only to have a hand grasp my arm. It's not Beefcake. This hand is gentler, but still firm. I whip my head up to see Rowan's look-alike, Kronan.

"Stay where you are. You aren't within the transmission's parameters anyway."

His voice is whisper soft and less rigid than the real Rowan's. But there's no mistaking the similarities now that he's standing so close.

"Am I addressing Queen Ursa?" Rowan asks. His hands brace what looks like a desk that has also come through the holographic transmission. The entire image goes grainy before re-stabilizing.

"You are." She descends the steps, and a small orb set atop a slim pillar near her throne follows her movement. A second, twin orb projects the image of Rowan and the others.

"Have you been in contact with Volkron One, the Sovereign's ship in the city called Tokyo?" he asks next.

I shift my arm and Kronan releases me. But he doesn't move away. He stays right where he is, and I know he'll grab me again if I try to enter whatever parameters the orb is transmitting to Rowan.

"I have not," Queen Ursa replies. "My business on Earth does not concern the Sovereign."

I note that they're speaking English, and I wonder why. Because of me? Does he even know yet that I'm here instead of in my room, where he left me?

Rowan leans forward over the desk. "What *is* your business here? You took Volkron. It is yours. Why have you followed the Volkranians to their new planet?"

Their new planet. I'm not a Salvager in the least, but Rowan calling Earth their new planet bothers me. This planet is not *theirs.*

The warden and the rest of the Volkranians have only ever told the human population that their planet had been laid to waste by a biological enemy. A parasite had destroyed Volkron, and the Volkranians had fled with the intention of saving what they could of their species.

But I know the truth.

A trickle of panic drips into my stomach again. The Volkranians, who are exponentially more powerful and advanced than humans, had been beaten. And these are their vanquishers.

The queen stops moving and stands with regal calm. "If you want to know why we are here, why do you not ask the Inoori slave standing at your side?"

I cut my eyes to the hologram and see the warden's chin lift a fraction of an inch. His silvery purple eyes flash.

"Slave?" I whisper.

"I was never *Inoori*," the warden growls through gritted teeth.

"No. You descend from a species of inept, feral beings—"

"*Enough.*" Rowan's voice breaks over Queen Ursa, silencing her. "He is a valuable and high-ranking officer of my fleet, no matter what his status was when the Inoori arrived on Volkron."

I stare at the warden and the strange scars that mark his face as he glares mercilessly at Queen Ursa. So far, he's the only Volkranian I've seen with the markings: two upside-down Js, surrounded by four circular impressions. Deliberate scarring. And now it sounds as if he had arrived on Volkron with the Inoori, as a slave.

"I urge caution," Queen Ursa says, her clasped hands, once calm, now turning into a stranglehold. "No matter what rank he has ascended to among the Volkranian people, he is, and will always be, a traitor."

"My loyalty never rested with you, and you were a fool to believe it would," the warden barks. "You dare call *my* people inept?"

Suddenly, I'm one hundred percent more interested in the warden. Talk about bad blood.

"Your history with the warden is not relevant. I want an answer, Queen Ursa. Why are you here?" Rowan demands.

She unclamps her hands and makes them into fists at her sides. "On the contrary. My history with your warden is more relevant than I am sure you have any knowledge of."

Another Volkranian, one I don't know, enters the hologram.

He speaks directly into Ash's ear. Ash straightens her spine and pushes down her shoulders before moving to Rowan's side to whisper to him.

I'm pretty certain I know what it's about.

Ash hasn't even finished speaking when Rowan pushes away from the desk. His image swells as he rushes the camera or orb or whatever it is that's capturing his image. Soon, the desk and the others aren't visible. He breathes evenly, a flare of temper in the flicker and snap of his irises, where a storm brews lightning.

"You've taken a human aboard your ship," he says, his fury barely contained. "Why?"

The queen remains cool and impassive, though I suspect she's doing a mental victory dance right about now. "I would like you to come to Avorra," she says. "We must speak, and the charming Penelope is—"

"Bait! Don't listen to her!" I shout. I'm tired of being quiet. Kronan takes my arm again tightly, like he thinks I'm going to make a run for the orb.

"Incentive," the queen finishes saying, without glancing my way, "for you to come with utmost haste."

I can't see him or the others, but the warden immediately, and vocally, refuses the suggestion. A roar of heated opinions rise up loudly behind Rowan. He speaks over them.

"The Sovereign has not granted me authority to negotiate with an enemy leader." It sounds as if he's reading straight from an intergalactic rulebook that sits in every control room in every spaceship.

"Of course he has not. But let me remind you, we are alone in this aegis dome. The humans cannot come to your aid, even should they wish to. Neither can your fellow Volkranians. I suggest you set aside procedure and do as I request."

Rowan doesn't ask what will happen if he refuses. He won't

give her that, and I'm glad. I don't exactly want to hear the ultimatum.

Rowan's eyes don't lower in contemplation. He doesn't turn away to consult with the others. He only lifts his chin another inch and stares down Queen Ursa.

"Instruct your artificers to prepare for my craft's arrival."

The holographic transmission cuts out.

No. Doesn't he get it? He's walking into a trap. He's giving himself up! If I were in that room with the other Volkranians, I'd be shouting and arguing with him to stop and think and to let the Inoori have the human.

But he isn't. Rowan is coming for me. Just like they knew he would.

CHAPTER NINE

Almost immediately, more Inoori step through the arched portal. The electric hum, buzz, and snap of blue plasma pops out people dressed in either gowns, or long tunics and straight-legged trousers, all in shades of red, green, and blue. They look like regular people. Tall people, like the Volkranians.

While a few of them have what Hollywood make-up crews used to imagine as distinctly alien features—like sharply cut cheekbones and brow bones, and skin in opaque shades of pearl and green and orange—they mostly look human. Bipedal and upright with skin and hair, though some are bald. I don't see anyone that looks like the warden, with his scarring and pale skin and violet eyes, so I figure none of the Inoori coming through the portal are slaves.

Kronan keeps a firm hold on my arm. I try to wrench it free with zero results. "What are you going to do to him?"

He slides his cold, unmoved gaze to me. "I would not harm my brother."

I go still, my arm limp in his grip. He doesn't just *look* like Rowan.

"You're his brother?" I ask. "He really is a prince?"

Rowan believed he'd been lied to, and if this is true, his whole *life* has been a lie.

His brother's face remains as expressive as a brick wall.

On the dais, Queen Ursa has taken her throne again. Her glare latches onto me. It makes me feel the same way I did when I fell through thin ice in my local park's pond years ago. I'd plunged through, and though the shallow, icy water had only reached to my knees, my whole body had prickled with stabbing cold.

"Are you his older brother or younger brother?" I ask, thrilling a little at the shift in his posture. I'm annoying him. *Good.*

He takes a full breath, his chest rising, but he doesn't answer. Instead, he shoves me to the side, toward the base of the steps leading up to the dais. The room has filled, though nowhere near capacity. Still, there are at least a hundred or more Inoori standing patiently. They've divided themselves into two groups the way people at a church wedding might. The bride's family on one side, the groom's family on the other. It leaves a narrow strip of open floor down the center, ending at the arched portal.

"I advise you to hold your tongue when Prince Torrin arrives," Kronan says, his voice low.

Prince Torrin. *That's* the name Goggles had said in the junkyard behind Sam's garage.

Sam. By now, he must have reached the hospital and told my mom what had happened. By now, she's probably explained everything about Rowan and last October.

"I'll speak when I want to," I say, and tug my arm again, if only to prove I'm not ready to back down.

"Do so and you will quickly learn the Inoori have no patience for what you claim as the right to free speech."

Great. Kim Jong-un over here has brushed up on his United States history.

There isn't time to argue. The quivering snap of blue plasma drags my eyes to the arched portal.

Rowan steps through, flanked by several Inoori males. His eyes immediately find me, but he only holds my stare for a moment. His eyes shift to his Inoori brother and the hand still gripping my arm. They then jump to the queen on her throne. He isn't armed, but the resolute glare he levels her with as he stalks down the open strip of floor feels like a weapon on its own.

Beside me, his brother bows his head. Around us, the crowds of Inoori bow their heads and bend forward at the hip, all looking like Prince Charming when he meets Cinderella.

Even on this ship, Rowan gets the royal treatment.

Only this time, unlike when the Volkranians angled their heads to him, he takes notice. Looking uncomfortable and unimpressed, he continues toward the base of the steps. He comes to a halt, five or so easy strides away from me.

"The warden has confessed everything," he says the moment he comes to a stop. "I am an Inoori prince that he stole, under directives from the former fleet commandant of Volkron Six, in the hours before the mass evacuation from Volkron."

The roomful of Inoori return to their standing positions as Rowan's voice carries into the high ceilings. If the queen had sails, they'd be limp, with the wind taken out of them. She hitches her chin, her expression cool.

"You seem to have made peace with the truth rather quickly," she comments.

"My peace does not matter. There are negotiations to begin."

I want Rowan to look at me, just once, but I know he can't. He can't show any weakness. Or maybe he really doesn't care that his whole life has been a lie. Maybe those things don't matter to Volkranians, or Inoori.

"What are your proposed terms?" he asks the queen.

"I have none. I want but one thing—my son, returned to me."

"I am a Volkranian. I do not belong among Inoori."

"You belong with your true people," the queen counters.

"The Volkranians *are* my people." An edge of annoyance works itself into his tone this time.

Queen Ursa remains quiet for a few moments, her hands clasped in her lap.

"I have spent many years following the Volkranian fleets along the Band, my only objective being to retrieve the child that was stolen from me," she says, and for the first time, real emotion burns through all that ice: sadness. Anger.

Rowan must hear it, too, because he softens his reply. "What the warden did was reprehensible, as was the former fleet commandant's order. It was borne out of a need for revenge."

The first fleet commandant had been a half-crazed, power-hungry maniac. It doesn't surprise me to hear he'd ordered a baby prince stolen from its cradle—or whatever piece of furniture Inoori babies use.

"Avorra is the only Inoori ship that has entered Earth's solar system," Rowan says. "Where are the rest of your people?"

Rowan pays the onlookers no mind. I'm wondering, however, if these are all the Inoori traveling with the queen. For such an enormous ship, this crowd seems a little anti-climatic. There are more men than women, and no children. They look dignified and stately themselves. Maybe this is like Queen Ursa's royal court. Could the peasants be elsewhere on the ship?

"They are on Volkron, of course," she answers.

"You left them?" he says.

To find *him*. She'd sacrificed twenty years traveling the Band...for rejection? She's not my favorite person ever but...*ouch.*

"Of course I did. You are my son. My prince."

Beside me, Kronan stiffens. I can practically smell the bitterness rolling off him. He's a prince, too, but clearly not firstborn. Double ouch.

"I am fleet commandant of Volkron Six." Rowan's brows pull together, and a muscle tenses along his jaw. "I am not your prince."

There is a rustle of shock through the crowd. So far, they haven't reacted to anything that has been said. This, however, seems to bowl them right over.

"You are my son." The queen's dismay cracks over each word. "You belong with us."

He won't meet her pleading gaze. Rowan's attention shifts to me, and I take a breath. My lungs fill, my heart swells, and it feels like my whole body sways toward him.

"Why have you brought Penelope into this?" he asks.

Incentive. That's what Queen Ursa said I was, and now I understand what she meant. He wouldn't be here if it weren't for me.

"Our emissaries aboard numerous Volkranian fleets have reported that she is your human consort," she answers.

I swing my head toward her, a blush rising on my cheeks. "What? No, I'm not—"

"How many of your spies are aboard our ships?" Rowan interrupts.

For the first time, his brother speaks. "That is not for you to know. You've made it clear you reject your Inoori blood."

The queen raises her hand in a command for him to be silent.

"Your brother, Kronan, suggested the presence of your consort might influence your decision to return to your family."

I send Kronan the Barbarian a glare. "I'm not his *consort*."

Consort implies that we are a couple. That I'm his companion. His mistress. We've only kissed.

And then he'd disappeared for seven months.

"Kronan was mistaken." Rowan turns his shoulders to indicate he's talking to Kronan but doesn't bother to meet his eyes. It's a cool dismissal. "I will return Penelope to her family, and then we can meet to discuss what happens next. The Volkranians' aim is for peace. I am certain the Sovereign will welcome Avorra if he has your pledge of non-violence."

The queen laughs, a tinkling sound, like glass beads chiming together until they shatter. "Oh, we do not plan to stay. This planet is dying. You forget that the Band travels backward through the time vortex. Earth is mere centuries away from complete self-destruction. Settling here is out of the question."

Everything she just said punches me right in the face. It feels like my brain is rattling around inside my skull. They know when Earth is going to self-destruct?

"We will return to Volkron," she adds. This time, it's Rowan who looks like he's been sucker punched.

"That is impossible. The Band travels in one direction."

"Perhaps for your Volkranian ships. However, Avorra is equipped for a backward trajectory," she replies with a careless shrug of one shoulder. "Now, enough of this. There will be no more discussion. When you boarded this ship, you were well aware that you would not be leaving it. We must prepare for departure."

Queen Ursa stands from her throne. It could just be the heavy beating of my heart and the blood rushing through my ears as panic sets in, but it sounds and looks like every other Inoori in the room takes a step in reverse.

We can't be leaving.

I'm still here. So is Rowan.

"Negotiations are not over," Rowan says, his voice deepening in resonance. He's getting angry, and considering he's usually able to conceal his emotions, it makes me shiver with dread. "I came aboard Avorra to discuss your terms, not bow down to them."

"My terms are simple," Queen Ursa replied. "You remain on Avorra willingly and return to Volkron with your true people...or I will have my guards incapacitate you and kill your consort, and then Avorra's weapons will destroy everyone and everything within the aegis dome."

Equal urges to scream and vomit nearly bring me to my knees.

"You would sacrifice millions of innocent lives," Rowan states.

"They mean nothing to me," Queen Ursa answers lightly.

Rowan holds her stare another few moments, and when he comes to the same conclusion that I already have—that she isn't bluffing, that she had won the moment Rowan agreed to come aboard her ship—he nods his head once.

Kronan nudges me forward. The other Inoori who'd flanked Rowan through the arched portal bow and then gesture for their returned prince to begin walking.

Rowan obeys, holding his broad shoulders in a rigid line. Kronan and I fall into step behind him.

"I'm so sorry, I shouldn't have let that healer into my room," I say to Rowan's straight back.

"You could not have known she was a spy," he replies without looking over his shoulder at me.

I guess not. I mean she'd passed for a loyal Volkranian for twenty years, right? But still. If I'd just kept my door shut and sucked up the pain the chip in my arm was blasting out, we wouldn't be here on Avorra, facing a trip out of Earth's atmosphere and onto the Band.

I seriously hope Rowan has a plan. He can't just submit to what Queen Ursa wants.

"Where are you taking him?" I ask Kronan.

"*I* am not taking him anywhere," he replies, his hand on my arm.

"Don't be so literal." I jerk my chin to the guards flanking Rowan. "Where are *they* taking him?"

"Penelope, do not concern yourself with me," Rowan says.

"He is correct," Kronan adds. "Your status as consort does not afford you such privileged information."

I crane my head to glare up at Kronan's profile. "For the last time—I am *not* his consort."

Kronan drags me to a halt and when he turns to loom over me, I can see whatever thin amount of patience he possessed has fled. "Then you are no longer valuable to us."

My heart stammers out another two beats, maybe three, before Rowan stops and turns. "You no longer have any authority to threaten her."

Kronan takes a reluctant step in reverse, and I let out a shuddering breath.

"Is Avorra equipped with escape transports?" Rowan asks.

Kronan nearly growls, "Of course."

"Now that I've agreed to stay, as your prince, you will heed my command. Return Penelope safely to her family."

"Rowan—"

Kronan cuts me off. "My pleasure, my prince," he drawls, taking a mocking bow.

Rowan's eyes meet mine. In the split second before he steps through the plasma portal, I see the honesty he'd shown me when we'd been alone, in my room aboard the new Volkron Six. The flicker of remorse, of pain and longing. Kronan is too busy taking an exaggerated and sarcastic bow to see, but it burns into me—and then Rowan is gone, vanishing in the blue snap of plasma.

Kronan straightens up and pulls me through next. Again, my body feels like it's bulging and stretching, and when we come out on the other side, Rowan isn't anywhere in sight.

Kronan jerks me through a busy worm-like corridor, swarms of Inoori people rushing toward us and past us. They're preparing for something. Lift off?

"*Rowan*," he says, his voice hard. "That is not his name."

No. Torrin is. *Prince* Torrin. The prince part doesn't surprise me, really, but it's difficult thinking of him with a different name.

Then again, if I'm shuttled off in an escape transport before Avorra takes flight with Rowan still onboard, it won't matter. He'll be gone for good this time.

I can't think about that. I can't give up.

My feet begin to feel less like awkward Minecraft blocks and more like actual feet as we walk swiftly down a second corridor.

"I know that Row—that *Prince Torrin* told you to take me to the ground, but—"

"He did not say that," Kronan cut in.

"Yes, he did. He told you to take me to my family."

A sinking sensation attacks my gut as we turn into another busy corridor.

"That is exactly what I am doing," Kronan says and then he grinds to a stop. His hand passes over a black, oval plate on the wall. The wall disappears, evaporating like mist to reveal another room. Kronan pushes me inside and I stumble forward, trying not to fall.

"Pen!"

My mom's voice barrels into my ears. I gasp, look up, and

there she is, running toward me, her arms open. She's wearing her rainbow polka dot scrubs, and I cling to her, confusion hot in my chest.

"What—?"

Over her shoulder, Hayden's round blue eyes stare up at me. Ice cold prickles rush in to drown my hot confusion.

An arm wraps around Hayden, pulling her back. *Sam.* He stares at me with fear and fury. Definitely more fury than fear, though.

I spin around. Kronan stands within the open wall space, the corridor still packed with Inoori foot traffic. "What have you done?"

"I have brought you to your family, as ordered." He gestures toward them with a smug tug of his lips.

"They haven't done anything! Take us back to the ground!"

"Pen," my mom warns in a whisper, her hands clutching my shoulders.

I shake them off and approach Kronan. "What do you want?"

His Inoori thugs had rounded up my mom, Sam, and Hayden and brought them here. But why?

Kronan takes the last step that separates us, and I have to hike my chin to glare up at him. He's just as tall as Rowan and just as intimidating. I *should* be afraid. He isn't Rowan. He doesn't care about me in the least. But I want answers.

"What I want is not important. It never has been," he adds, nostrils flaring. "But my queen insists on a peace offering with my brother. And you should be thankful."

But...she doesn't *need* to make a peace offering to Rowan. He's agreed to travel with them, even if it will be under duress.

"Thankful?" Sam shouts from behind me. "For abducting us?"

Kronan lifts his eyes to Sam. "For saving your species." He

drops his attention back to me. "You heard my queen. This planet will not survive another five hundred years. However, bringing human subjects to a new planet will at least ensure the species will."

I balk at him, my jaw unable to close. "She wants to resettle humans on Volkron?"

Kronan cocks his head and stares at me for a moment, like I'm wrong, or being stupid. "We will have a need for laborers," Kronan replies. "Humans will do nicely."

Laborers? My mind clicks to the warden and what the queen had called him. *Slave.* He hadn't been Inoori, he'd said. He'd been taken from his planet. Made into a slave.

My mom makes a noise like a whimper, and I turn around to find Sam's other arm around her shoulders, holding her close. Hayden continues to stare at Kronan in rapt horror. Her expression makes me want to shove and punch and claw our way to freedom. But how?

I spin back to face Kronan. "You can't restart a species with *four* humans."

He snorts and shakes his head as he backs out through the gap in the wall, into the corridor. "It is no wonder your whole planet will perish."

Kronan passes his palm over the oval plate and with that, the wall reappears. It looks solid, and when I pound my fists against it, it feels solid. There are no other doors or windows, just lights along the ceiling. I turn back to my mom and Sam. Hayden's face is now buried in his stomach and she's trembling.

"You," Sam seethes. "*You* did this."

CHAPTER TEN

My lungs suddenly shrink to the size of acorns. He's right. They're here because of me. Because of Rowan and those two days in October when everything had changed forever.

"No, Sam," my mom tries to say, but he talks over her.

"I brought you into my home. Trusted you."

"I...I didn't think it mattered anymore," I say, even though I know everything that comes out of my mouth is going to sound like an enormous pile of horse manure to him. "He was gone. Or at least I thought he was and there was no reason the Volkranians would ever talk to me again, or search for me."

"Rowan." Sam spits the name like it's a joke. My mom must have told him everything. "Your alien boyfriend."

"Stop it," I say, my temper rising. "Arguing isn't going to help us. We need to get out of here."

I start to walk the perimeter of the room, looking for anything that could help. Another exit. A button to push. *Anything*. I find an oval plate like the one Kronan had passed his hand over.

"There is no way out," Sam barks. "This isn't the goddamned movies. And *that*—" he says when I swipe my palm over the oval plate. The wall disappears, simply vanishes, to reveal a smaller room. "—is a bathroom. Nice of them, right? At least we can piss in private."

He's angry. Okay. I get that. I'm angry, too, and scared and feeling guilty as hell. But this *cannot* happen.

"They must have taken more humans," I say, refusing to glance at Sam. "Did you see Kronan's expression? He was practically laughing at the idea of only taking four of us."

"Kronan?" my mom repeats. At least she doesn't sound like she'd like to bite my head off.

"Rowan's brother. Younger brother, I think. He's Inoori, like Rowan, though Rowan didn't know. He was stolen as a baby," I try to explain, but with every word, Sam's expression has darkened.

"I don't give a rat's ass what happened to poor Rowan," he says. "All I care about is getting Hayden to safety."

He sends a soft, apologetic glance to my mom. Good. At least he's only a little angry with her for keeping my secrets.

"I thought you were the one saying there was no way out," I reply.

"Yeah, well, didn't you hear The Wrath of Khan over there? Us humans make good laborers. So let's get to work."

He scans the dark gray walls, running his hands over them and feeling for God knows what. I go into the bathroom and start doing the same thing. There's a toilet bowl, kind of like the one on Volkron Six I once used. A standing urinal that a person is supposed to straddle. There's a sink, a counter, and even a wastebasket.

My eyes trip over it.

On Volkron Six, the wastebasket in Rowan's bathroom had been a kind of automatic laundry chute. He'd tossed a used towel into the basket and the bottom had opened and sucked the towel down before sealing again.

I don't see any towels or toilet paper, and the sink counter is bare as well.

"Sam," I call out. "Mom. Do either of you have a piece of paper, or something to throw away?"

They enter the bathroom, their eyes narrowed. Hayden peeks around the corner, too.

"Why?" Sam asks.

I hold out my hand. "I want to try something."

He sighs and reaches into his back pocket. "A couple quarters," he says, handing them over.

At least he isn't skewering me with a hateful glare. I hold them over the laundry chute and let them go. The two coins clink against the tin-sounding floor of the chute. And sit there.

"Never mind. I thought—"

The floor drops and sucks down the quarters. The flaps fly back together, and the sucking sound is gone. The quarters are, too.

"Where does that lead?" Sam asks, immediately catching on to my idea. My really awful, terrifying, and stupid idea.

"I don't know," I answer, my heart already throbbing. "I think it's a laundry chute."

"No," my mom says. "It's too dangerous. We don't know where it leads, or if there's even any breathable air in there. Did you hear it? It's a pneumatic system."

Like the module elevators aboard the cityship. A fast tube-like system. This one might dump the contents into either a trash receptacle or a laundry room of sorts.

Or an incinerator.

"And what do we even do if we come through alive? We're on a spaceship in the air. We have no way of getting back down to the ground," my mom goes on, her Voice of Reason hat pulled firmly down around her ears.

"What do we do instead? Sit in here waiting to be taken to another solar system and made into slaves?" Sam asks.

I agree with both of them. We can't sit and wait, but we also can't keep going without a plan.

"We have to find Rowan."

Sam slaps me with another death glare and Hayden gasps in alarm. I hold up my hands to her. "He would never hurt us. We can trust him. If he knows there are humans aboard Avorra, he'll bargain for our release."

"Trust him?" Sam's shout bounces around the small room and batters my eardrums. "He's one of them!"

"No! He only agreed to join them because Queen Ursa promised to destroy everything inside the weird dome that's over New York right now, including the Volkranian cityship."

She'd promised to kill me, too. But I don't say that. There's no point in worrying my mom anymore than she already is.

"So he's just protecting his own kind."

"And don't forget the millions of *humans* under the dome," I add.

"Fine. If you want to wait to be saved by your alien boyfriend, go for it. But I'm not."

Sam puts his foot inside the wide mouth of the chute.

"No!" I scream in unison with Hayden and my mom.

"Take care of Hayden," Sam says, and with a look just for her, adds, "I'll get us out of here. Trust me, okay?"

"You're crazy! Stop!" I shout, but the floor flaps drop, and in a blink, Sam's gone. He's sucked through the hole in the floor and he's just...gone.

"Sam!" Hayden screams, panic choking the one syllable into a sob.

"That idiot!" I know I sound angry, and I am. I'm pissed. But I'm also scared. I want to scream and cry the same way Hayden is, her face buried in my mom's stomach now that her big brother has gone and jumped into a tubing system that might kill him.

Because of me. They wouldn't have ever been targeted by the Inoori if not for me.

"What do we do?" my mom asks, her hands running over Hayden's long brown hair in an attempt to soothe her, even though her own eyes glisten with tears.

"I have no idea." My heart thumps erratically. Fast, then slow. Then fast again. I feel sick. Dizzy.

"Pen," my mom says, but it sounds like her voice is coming through a long tunnel. A tunnel filled with whistling wind.

What if Sam can't breathe? What if the tubing system constricts and he's stuck somewhere inside of it, without air? Or if he's dropped a thousand feet with nothing to catch him?

"Pen, sit down." I do what my mom commands. I crash onto my knees and close my eyes, my chest flashing hot then cold. What has Sam done? What have *I* done?

"You're going to faint," my mom warns, but I shake my head. I can't faint. I'm not going to be that damsel in distress. Sam had told me to go ahead and wait for Rowan to rescue me, but that's not my plan. It never has been. I need to find Rowan— and that means getting out of this room.

I open my eyes and look at the chute.

"No." My mom must have seen something in my eyes. Or maybe my body language had given something away.

"I know," I say, but I'm still thinking it—until voices sound from the other room. It's not a language I recognize. What language do the Inoori speak? Inoorian? They're barking out their words, whatever language it is.

I force myself to stand, refusing to be found on my knees. I'm just in time. Two jacked-up Inoori guys storm into the bathroom. Neither of them is Kronan.

"Where is the male?" one asks. They're both uniformed in

gray, black, and red tunic-type shirts and black boots. Each of them wears the same wireless headsets the Inoori on the soccer field had been wearing.

My mom and I exchange a glance. Hayden stares with saucer eyes at the aliens.

"Our systems have reported an unidentified object in the second level waste ducts," the other alien says, his eyes going to the chute.

They have sensors in there. *Of course.* And it's a trash removal system after all.

The alien touches the earpiece in his right ear. "The male is missing." A pause. Then, "Yes, Your Excellency."

The alien drops his finger from the earpiece and turns his attention to me. "You. Come with us." Anticipating my refusal, he takes my arm and tugs me from the bathroom.

"Leave her alone!" my mom shouts, but I'm already being dragged away, and they aren't going to stop on her command.

I twist around to see her and Hayden following. "It's okay. I'll be okay."

It's total bull. I have no idea if I'll be okay. But just like Sam had put on a brave face before leaping to his possible death, I try to do the same thing.

The alien leading me away cinches his grip around my forearm, right where the dematerializer chip has been implanted.

"Watch it." I wriggle my arm. "That hurts."

The alien loosens his grip enough to dull the pain. I guess he could have been a jerk and gripped my arm tighter.

"Where are we going?" I don't expect an answer. We've walked through the disappearing wall and into the corridor, and we're coming up on another one of those arched portals. They're clearly able to transport people from one place on Avorra to another.

"You are too much of a risk," the alien leading me says,

surprising me with an answer. "His Excellency believes you will follow the foolhardy male into the waste ducts."

"Where do they lead? Is he okay?"

He doesn't answer, but when I look up at him, I see amusement on his mouth. The other alien wears the same expression. *Oh no.*

"Is he dead?" I can't breathe.

They pull me through the portal, and after the bulge and snap of my vision, we're spit out on the other side, into a field of what looks like wheat. Instead of a sky overhead, there are endless rows of bright solar-like panels emitting harsh UV light. It even smells like a field, all sweet soil and rain.

We begin to walk through the vast field. The stalks are on my right, and to my left there is nothing but a tall, black metal wall with a grid of spouts. A few jet out a fine mist.

"Tell me what's happened to him," I say, my arm brushing against the stalks of wheat as we walk quickly. It rustles off a strange, pungent smell.

"He should not be dead," the Inoori man finally replies, still clearly amused.

Thank God. I release my pent-up breath and look into the wall of wheat beside me. The field seems never ending—until the aliens drag me to the left, toward a door. It slides open, they push me through, and then the door slides shut again.

I whip around, but they're gone.

I turn and face a big, windowless, silver-walled room with dozens of panels of blinky lights and buttons and levers. I feel like I've been thrown in an airlock, though. There is no sound at all except for my own heavy breathing.

And then footsteps.

Kronan enters the room from an open archway to my left, and immediately pins me with a glare. His square jaw sets as he goes to one of the panels on the wall and starts pressing buttons.

"If you think this changes anything, you are mistaken," Kronan says without a glance in my direction. "Avorra will find your human friend and my Divitrix will transmit his location within moments."

"Divitrix?"

He sighs loudly and taps the back of his ear. I take a closer look. The barest shimmer of light flickers from behind the shell of his ear, underneath his skin.

"What is that?" I ask.

"Avorra's bio-retinal intelligence system." He twists a dial, again refusing to look at me. "All Divitrix receive a steady feed from the system."

"Oh," I reply, rubbing my forearm and the disc there. I wonder what other kinds of under-the-skin tech there are on Avorra.

"How can I convince you to let us go?" I ask. There must be something I can say or do. "What is it that you want?"

A humming sensation tickles up through my feet. The floor is vibrating.

"Your freedom is behind you," he replies, his face turned toward the panels. "And I want nothing you can offer."

"You are such an asshole." It slips out from between my lips as easily as a breath of air. I know it's stupid the moment I hear myself saying it. I've made a mistake.

Kronan spins away from the panels, stalks up to me, and wraps his hand around my throat. He shoves me against a wall, proving that yes, I have definitely pushed too far.

He isn't squeezing my throat hard enough to cut off my air supply, but his grip is firm. He brings his face to within inches of mine, his sky blue and moss green eyes boring into me.

"Your insolent tongue is going to get you killed." He pushes harder against my throat, *now* making it more difficult to breathe. I kick at his legs, but he pins my thighs into place with his knees. "Consider this a warning. My queen is not as forgiving as I am. And when Prince Torrin is awakened, he will not stand for it, either."

I stop trying to wrestle free. Heat fills my cheeks, my eyes watering, my ears throbbing with the blood Kronan's grip isn't allowing to flow freely through my veins. But I'm not worried about blacking out. I'm worried about what he's just said.

"Awakened?" I rasp, choking on my word as I force it past his grip.

He releases me, and I suck in air. He really is an asshole, but hell if I'm going to say it out loud again.

"He was born Inoori, and like every other Inoori, he was given a Divitrix," he replies, still peeved.

The fingers that had just been constricting my air flow go back to fiddling with buttons and levers. "It's not just a device that lets us communicate with Avorra's Eye. It's as important to an Inoori as blood and air. It's our history, our language, our world."

Avorra's Eye. It sounds like a ship-wide security system— and all-knowing search engine. The skin around my throat feels bruised and my ears are still ringing, but I'm not anywhere near passing out.

"He has been asleep for most of his life," Kronan explains. "Once he is awakened, he will no longer be Volkranian."

Rowan has a device behind his ear. A device that has been turned off since he was a baby. And when the Inoori turn it back on...he'll no longer be the Rowan I know?

My stomach turns and my throat closes off. It's not nausea, but sadness. I don't want him to change. I don't want him to become like Kronan or Queen Ursa.

"The Divitrix can change the way he thinks? The way he feels?" I ask.

Kronan curls his lip at my question. "The Divitrix will make certain he *doesn't* feel."

He turns around and goes back toward the panels. The floor is still humming, and I realize something.

"Are we moving?"

"If your male friend had not foolishly injected himself into Avorra's waste ducts, yes, we would be moving. The system has locked down until he can be extracted." Kronan continues farther into the room, which curves to the left and out of sight.

"Why is the floor vibrating then?"

Kronan disappears around the corner. His voice sounds from the other side of the room.

"The ducts that feed the hartsheaf fields are closing off in preparation for ascension."

The field of wheat the guards led me through. They call it hartsheaf? Good to know for when they make us slaves and demand we work the fields on Volkron. *As if.*

I storm forward, taking the left turn after him. "If you think humans are going to bow down to being slaves, you're wrong. We'd rather die than live that way."

I pull up short. This part of the room is bracket-shaped and obviously a bedroom. The bed isn't as utilitarian as the one in Rowan's room on Volkron Six, but it's not straight out of IKEA either. The frame is metal, the mattress flat and covered in a solid white blanket, but there are at least four pillows instead of the single, kidney-bean one Volkranians like to drug themselves with.

Kronan is filling a cup with clear liquid from a tap in the wall. "Laborers. Not slaves," he says.

"You called the warden a slave."

"My queen called him that."

"So you *do* have slaves."

"I did not order you brought to me so that I could converse

with you," he growls after draining the liquid from the cup in one long gulp.

"Then why did you?"

He slams the cup on a shelf set into the wall and it's whisked away in a blink of an eye.

"Because I did not trust that you wouldn't do something as idiotic as your male friend."

"And so what if I had? What do you care?"

"You are a gift to the prince," he replies, sitting on the edge of the bed. "Dead consorts do not make very impressive gifts."

I don't have a comeback for that one. I've already insisted I'm not Rowan's consort, but it won't do any good. Their spies, whoever they were, have told them differently.

I need to get out of here and find Rowan. I have to get back to my mom and Hayden, and it would be really great if I could find out if Sam has been pulled out of their waste duct system yet.

"What now?" I ask as Kronan rubs his forehead, as if he'd like to go to sleep. And no sooner do I think it than he starts to unlace his boots.

"Your friend will be extracted, and then we will ascend from Earth's atmosphere. The journey to the Band should take four of your earthly hours."

He lines up his boots next to his bed and lays back. I stand there, staring at him, wishing I had a pillow to chuck at his head. Then again, it would likely have him leaping up and strangling me for a second time.

"You're seriously going to sleep?"

"Yes."

I wait and think, my eyes traveling behind me, toward the curve in the room. There are two doors back there. I could try to slip out if—

"This room is sealed. Only my Divitrix can open the doors," he says.

"What, did your Divitrix read my mind, too?" I ask, my hope sinking like lead.

"It cannot read minds. You are simply obvious."

He still has his eyes shut, an arm thrown up over his eyes to block the light.

"So what, I'm supposed to stand here for three hours and watch you sleep?"

I shift side to side. Man. I need a bathroom. I haven't peed in hours.

"Sitting is also an option," Kronan replies.

How hospitable of him. "Just let me see Rowan."

"You will be presented to the prince once we clear Earth's atmosphere and begin ascending to the Band."

His voice is dull. Remote and empty. He'd said the Divitrix would ensure Rowan doesn't feel at all. Is that how every Inoori is? Unfeeling? Volkranians give off an unfeeling vibe too, but theirs is more like unswerving loyalty to duty and precision and perfectionism, while so far the Inoori vibe I'm getting is dismissive coldness.

"Do you have a bathroom?"

He lets out an enormous sigh, full of frustrated annoyance, and leaps off the bed. I back up a few steps, both afraid and happy to see at least some emotion from him. So maybe they aren't completely unfeeling.

He wings a hand over a black disc on the wall and an entrance appears. "Do not attempt to jump into the waste ducts. I promise that it will be far less pleasant than having to sit in my chambers for the next few hours."

I go inside the bathroom and the wall materializes, sealing me in and affording me some privacy. Maybe. This Divitrix thing is Avorra's Eye, so for all I know it could be spying on me while I pee. The toilet is easy to figure out, and once I'm finished and have also figured out how to wash my hands, I feel better prepared. Escaping on a full bladder would have been distracting.

I wave my hand over the oval disc on this side of the bathroom, but nothing happens. *Crud.*

"Hello?" I call out.

The wall immediately disappears, and Kronan is standing right where I'd left him. *What a creeper.* He'd listened to me pee? Here's hoping the magic walls are soundproof.

"I'm hungry," I say, and Kronan closes his eyes, suppressing, I'm sure, the urge to throttle me again. "What do you guys eat?"

He rubs the back of his neck and walks away.

"You have food we can consume, right? And water?"

The Volkranians hadn't. This is going to be a short ride if they don't, either.

Kronan opens a drawer in the wall and a cloud of vapor billows. He reaches in and brings out a small glass bottle with a silver cap.

"You can drink this," he says, handing me the bottle. The glass practically burns my hand it's so cold.

"What is it?" I ask, suspicious. But I'm also really thirsty. I twist open the cap and sniff.

"We have a limited supply of drinking water appropriate for humans onboard Avorra, but we have the capability to produce more," Kronan says.

I don't smell anything strange, so I take a tentative sip. It doesn't taste like anything, either. I take another sip.

"That, however, is not water," Kronan adds as the second glug of liquid is streaming down my throat.

I cough and shove the bottle back at him. "*What?*"

That's when I feel the sway of the floor and hear Kronan's muffled voice saying, "It will not harm you."

The room fragments, my vision breaking like a dropped mirror. The shards fly up and outward in slow motion. A black hole opens in the center of the room and as it gets bigger, my body starts to go numb. I have the vague sensation of hands on my legs and back before the last shards of my vision push beyond the boundaries of my sight, leaving me in total darkness.

"You...jerk," I whisper as the black hole pulls me in.

CHAPTER ELEVEN

When my eyes crack open, my fingers are still numb. The rest of me tingles, and within seconds I realize I'm lying down, my face mashed into a pillow. I bolt upright and recognize Kronan's room. I'm in his bunk. And he's nowhere in sight.

All sound is muffled, as if I'm underwater, and I hardly hear the rustle of his bed and blanket as I swing my prickly feet over the edge. The Inoori scumbag *drugged* me. Probably just to get me to shut up, but I do a quick once-over to make sure I'm still dressed, and that things don't feel...*off*. I'm okay though. I don't know a thing about Kronan really, but if I had money, I'd place a hefty bet on him *not* being a roofie rapist.

I stand up and take a few tentative steps before it hits me that I might have been out cold for a while. My pulse hammers in my neck. A cold sweat crackles over my back, between my shoulder blades.

"Kronan?" My voice parts the muffled quiet, and I'm not too surprised when there's no answer. I turn the corner, to where the panels of lights and switches and levers still blink and hum softly. What does Kronan do here in this room? It's where he sleeps...but does he operate some part of the ship from this spot, too? Something like the wheat—or hartsheaf—fields the two guards had walked me through?

It seems odd that Queen Ursa's son, a prince, would oversee some agricultural aspect of their ship—and live in what amounts to a boiler room. I walk closer to the panels and run my finger along the raised writing under some levers. It looks like Braille.

"You are finally conscious."

I spin toward his voice. Kronan stands within the entrance to another room I hadn't seen earlier.

"What did you give me to drink?" I ask, my tongue still a little heavy.

"A sedative." He enters the room, looking through me, as if my being there is still an annoyance.

"How long have I been asleep?" My brain feels like it's shedding a winter's worth of fur.

"Two hours."

Oh god. I look around, wanting a window. I want to look out and see New York City. The cloud covered sky.

"Did you find Sam?"

"Yes. As soon as you fell asleep."

"I didn't fall asleep! You knocked me out!" They found Sam. They launched. "Where are we?"

"Avorra is nearing the asteroid belt," he says.

"In outer space?"

"Of course in outer space," he scoffs.

We're in outer space. *I'm* in outer-*freaking*-space.

"Where is...Prince Torrin?" I remember his Inoori name at the last moment. It wins me a suspicious glance from Kronan.

"Busy."

My stomach knots, and a chill steals down my arms and spine. "So, his Divitrix thing...it's been turned on?"

Kronan doesn't reply, and I notice he has something in his hands. It's a long, metallic case, big enough for something like a guitar or a trombone. He brings it to a table and sets it on top. With a swipe of his hand over two locks, the case hisses open.

"You are to wear this," he says in the seconds before I see what's inside the long case. When I do, I taste a small amount of throw up on the back of my tongue.

It's a dress.

A sparkling golden dress, with a pair of matching heeled shoes.

"What the hell is that?" I blurt out. Kronan's eyes darken.

"Prince Torrin ordered his seamstresses to have this made for you to wear to tonight's feast."

Rowan has sent this dress to me? I don't believe Kronan. I bet the queen has had something to do with it. "We're feasting?"

"The Inoori do eat," Kronan replies, pulling the dress from the case. He chucks it at me. I bat the thing away from my face without letting it drop. I want to put the dress on as much as I want another drugged-up drink from Kronan, but that doesn't mean the gorgeous dress deserves to be thrown onto the floor.

"Hey, watch it," I say. "I'm sure this thing cost a lot of whatever money you guys use. And exactly *why* do I have to wear it?"

The material is the strangest texture I've ever felt. It's almost like holding weighted water. But I still don't want to put it on.

Kronan glowers at me again, looking pointedly at my jeans. "You cannot wear those clothes when you are presented to the prince."

I walk on unsteady feet to the table and put the dress back into the case, not half as neatly as it had been before. "I'm not dressing up for any feast. I want to see my mom and Sam, and I want to—"

"It is amusing that you would think you have a choice in anything." Kronan looks anything but amused as he grabs the dress in his large hand and shoves it at me again. "Do not make me summon help to get you dressed."

A blistering rash of insults lines up on my tongue, ready for launch. But I recall the squeeze of his fingers around my throat and his warning to curb my insolence, and I pin my lips together. I grab the dress, then the heels, and stalk toward the wall the bathroom had appeared behind earlier. It won't dissolve for me though.

I clear my throat, and Kronan comes up behind me. He waves his hand over the mounted plate. The wall smacks back into place as soon as I'm inside the bathroom. *Fine.* I'll wear this ridiculously beautiful gown, though I'm not sure how the seamstresses knew my measurements. But as I take off my jeans and shirt, I can't help but feel nauseated. Not just because I'm about to be presented like some kind of gift to their returned prince, but because I'm about to see Rowan again...and I'm terrified he'll be a stranger.

———

KRONAN IS GONE WHEN I STEP OUT OF THE BATHROOM. Instead, two more guards wait in the open doorway to the hartsheaf field. I'm not wearing the shoes yet. The heels are tall and spiked, like a pair of stilettos, and with my luck and skill, I'll break an ankle the second I try to walk in them.

So, in my bare feet, and carrying the shoes in my hand, I approach the steely-faced guards. Without a word, they step aside and gesture for me to exit Kronan's room. I walk ahead of them, feeling extremely self-conscious. The gown's material had felt like weighted water in my hands, and it still feels like a liquid layer. Almost like I'm walking around naked, though the dress covers everything that needs to be covered. Still, I don't like it. I want to be in my jeans. I want to be *home*.

One guard takes the lead, and we snap through the arched portal and into another corridor. I don't recognize it, but I suppose on a ship this size, there must be thousands of rooms and scores of levels. Wherever we are, it's warm, and I can hear the muted sound of many voices coming from a turn ahead in the corridor.

My bare feet, I notice, are walking on a type of soft surface, like suede, and I stop to put on my shoes. They're torture instruments, really, and once they're in place I'm about three inches taller. But I'm still much shorter than the guards, who've stopped to wait for me.

My stomach twists with nerves and for a second, I think I'll be sick. It could be any number of things: remnants of being drugged, the prospect of becoming a laborer on Volkron, the fact that I'm in outer space...maybe I'm even getting space sick. That's a thing, right? Astronauts sometimes have a hard time acclimating to lack of gravity. But there's plenty of gravity on Avorra, and as we approach the turn in the corridor and the voices get louder, I realize I'm mostly dreading that when I see Rowan, it's no longer going to be *Rowan*.

I make the turn and enter a large room filled with mirrors and lights and people. Well...Inoori "people." They're all dressed as elegantly as I am, and in some cases, even more so. Long gowns and robes of the brightest colors are worn by both men and women, and again, both men and women are dressed in crisp tunics and trousers too, all in varying shades of gray and black.

A pinkish hue reflects off everyone and everything, and little spheres of glowing lights drift lazily through the air, like string lights without the string. As I take the first few steps in, voices start to fall off. Like an ocean wave, attention rushes toward me. Once again, I feel naked.

Queen Ursa wears a crimson gown with an elaborate headpiece, like something Queen Amidala, from the three *Star Wars* movies everyone wishes had never been made, would have worn. She watches me with unmasked indifference, as if she is already bored by me.

A suited figure slides in front of her. It takes my brain a second to realize it isn't Kronan.

I've never seen Rowan in anything other than his black jumpsuit, and the dark gray tunic and trousers he now wears changes strange things about him, like his skin tone and hair color. His skin appears more bronzed than before; his hair seems like it's a matte brown instead of touched by golden strands. The clothing gives him a bulky, square-like shape, but it's the expression on his face that turns my blood into shards of ice. It matches the queen's perfectly.

The queen begins to speak, but I can't understand a word. It's clear she's talking to Rowan, though I can't see any reaction, either good or bad, in his expression. It's the same distant and flat indifference. Everyone is listening to whatever she is saying, and as soon as she stops, all attention pivots to Rowan.

His reply is brief, and it isn't in English either. He turns away from me almost immediately and slips back into the crowd. I stand there alone, as everyone else goes back to their mingling. I try to follow Rowan with my eyes, but I can't see him through the tall, bedazzled crowd. He'd just...walked away. He'd looked at me as if he were looking through me, and then turned his back.

A painful knot grows in my throat and a numbness trickles into my arms and legs. My feet ache from the shoes, and all I want to do is rip them off and fling them, heel first, at the queen's head. I won't though. I'm alone, and totally unprotected. Rowan is gone, woken up by his Divitrix just like Kronan had promised.

For the next few minutes, I stand in the same spot, my

clammy hands clasped in front of me, suffering from an acute case of wallfloweritis. A chiming sound strokes through the voices and laughter, and everyone begins to flow in the opposite direction. Across the room, an entrance leads to yet another space. I stay where I am, not sure if I can move without falling flat on my face. No one looks my way. I take a glimpse behind me. There aren't any guards positioned at the exit. If no one cares what I'm doing, maybe I could go find—

"Penelope."

I jump and the heel on my left foot collapses out from underneath me. I stumble to the side and just barely catch myself. It's Rowan, and he's looking at me again with those flat eyes. The blue and green irises are placid, the two colors almost completely unmixed.

He doesn't try to catch me or steady me, either.

"Rowan—"

"You will address me as Prince Torrin."

A fist the size of an Easter ham burrows into my stomach. Tears spring to my eyes, but I fight them back.

"Prince Torrin," I whisper. But I don't have anything left to say. I can't even look at him.

"I will see you after the feast," he says, and with a flick of his eyes over my shoulder, he walks away again.

The guards are back, herding me from the room and into the corridor. I yank off my heels and go barefoot, carrying the shoes and forcing my mind blank. I should be paying attention to where we're going and trying to figure out how the same portal arch that brought us here ends up popping us out somewhere else on the ship, no hartsheaf field in sight. The guards hadn't touched the archway, and yet they've led me into another muffled and warm corridor, almost like a hotel hallway. How does the portal know where they want to go?

I follow listlessly, not wanting to think, not wanting to fight.

A door slides open, and I'm directed inside a large living area, with curved, plush furniture and glossy, glass-like tables. An enormous window on the far side of the room bubbles out into a black expanse, pinpricked with silver. Outer space.

My heart slows and my stomach drops. It's my first look outside, and suddenly some strange pressure starts to squeeze my lungs. Deep inside my ears, I hear a sharp, monotonous ringing. That's not air out there. It's not a window that I'm looking through—it's a *shield*.

"Stay here," one guard orders from behind me.

I'm slow to turn, but when I do, the door seals shut, leaving me in here all alone. I drop the heels and wait a minute before going to the door. It doesn't open, and there aren't any buttons or switches that I can see that might open it.

Great. Another prison. Only this room...I look at it again... this room is *classy*. Considering Rowan said he'd see me after the feast, I'm guessing it's either his living space, or my own. The prince's consort might be given a nice place to live. Not that I want it.

I think of my mom and Sam and Hayden, and the muscles along my neck and back tense. I want to see them. My skin feels like it doesn't fit right, and I grit my teeth against the irritating, restless sensation. I'd rather be in that little holding room with them, than alone in here. At this point, I don't even want to see Rowan. Not if he's going to just look at me the way he had. Not if he's...not *him* anymore.

I walk through the room, careful not to touch anything. It's museum perfect, and I'd been trained a long time ago not to leave fingerprints or risk breaking anything that would cost my parents a small fortune to replace.

I poke my head into a few other entranceways, finding a bathroom, a bedroom, a large circular room with mirrored walls, a smaller room with desks and chairs, and another bubble window with a panic-attack-inducing view. As I enter each room, a light source that seems to be built into the corners of the walls turns on, and as I leave, the room fades to black.

I search for other doors, another way to escape, but there isn't anything. And really, where would I go? We're nearing the asteroid belt around Mars. A trip that would have taken a normal, human-led mission months to reach had taken Avorra a few *hours*.

I go back out into the main living area and plop down onto one of the couches, my head and chest both heavy with a terrifying reality: *There is no getting off this ship. There is no going home.* I bring up my legs and clasp my arms around them, leaning my forehead against my knees. *Breathe, Pen.* I can't panic. I can't. I still have my mom and Sam and Hayden, and I'm betting there are other humans aboard somewhere. If Queen Ursa's plan is to develop a species of human laborers on her planet, she'll have to have taken more of us.

I close my eyes and concentrate on breathing. On not crying and giving in to the wild panic clamoring to break free from the mental cage I've been keeping it in.

When I open my eyes again, it's to a sound. And I realize I'm laying on my side, a hand tucked under my cheek and my legs curled up. I'd fallen asleep. The groggy, dizzy feeling of waking up from a nap swarms me as I sit up.

I'm no longer alone.

Rowan stands just inside the living area, the door already sealed shut behind him. He stares at me, his brows furrowed and shoulders tense, and there's a split second when I forget.

"Rowan," I say, trying to stand. My feet are prickly, and my head feels light, so I sit back down.

"Prince Torrin," he corrects, heading straight for one of the other rooms. "It will be better for you if you remember my real name."

My brain catches up fast. Prince Torrin has been awakened. Rowan is gone.

A rush of anger spurts through my slack muscles. I force myself to my feet again, prickly soles and all, and take a few steps to follow him. He's gone into the circular room with mirrored walls. One of the mirrors disappears as he reaches forward. His hand looks like it's about to strike the mirror when it simply evaporates, revealing a closet. Clothing, like the stuff he's already wearing, hangs inside.

"Where are the other humans?" I ask. "My mom and Sam and Hayden. Where are you keeping them?"

He shrugs out of his tunic, leaving him bare from the waist up, and he hangs it inside the closet. I'd forgotten how defined he is; his abs sleek, his skin smooth and unblemished. With his back to me, I steal a look behind his ear. A pale blue light winks just underneath the skin. Just like Kronan's Divitrix.

"There is no need for you to concern yourself with them. As my consort you will have little contact with anyone but me."

My eyes burn. I don't know if the tears are from sadness or anger. Right then, with the spike in my pulse, I'm leaning toward anger.

"Has that blinky light behind your ear completely erased everything you already know about me?" I step inside the mirrored room as Rowan pulls out another shirt, this one a little more form fitting, and puts it on. "There is absolutely no chance in hell I'm going to sit around here being your pet. That Divitrix might have changed you, but it won't change me."

Finished dressing, he walks past me, back into the living area. He doesn't even look up.

"Kronan told you about the Divitrix," he replies.

I peer at his back, which he's consistently kept turned to me. Just like he had on the new Volkron Six. It had confused me then. Now, it tears at my heart. "How did you know that?"

"Avorra's Eye. It hears and sees everything that takes place on Avorra, and is connected to every Divitrix."

"So what, you can all read one another's minds? You can see everything everyone else does, and hear what they say?"

"No. Avorra's Eye chooses what it stores into its memory, and what it shares with others."

I digest that for a minute as Rowan walks toward the huge window looking out into space. I don't want to follow him, and not just because he's about as cold as a popsicle. I also don't need a closer look at the dark expanse outside the ship.

"Avorra's Eye is autonomous?" I ask. "It's...alive?"

"Artificially, yes."

And it feeds everyone who possesses a Divitrix a constant stream of selected information.

"What about right now, in here?" I ask. "Is Avorra's Eye listening to us?"

Rowan turns his head, showing me his profile. "It's always listening."

On Volkron Six, there had been monitors everywhere except for private living spaces. On transports, in the pneumatic modules, in every room and corridor. There had been a few times when Rowan would glare at me to remind me to keep quiet until we could be free from the monitors. Here, the monitor is with him permanently.

When he shifts fully to meet my gaze for the first time, I don't know what to say or think. The look is pointed and direct; it might even be meaningful. I try to think of ways we could possibly communicate without Avorra's Eye listening or watching. How do people communicate without sight or sound? I mean, take Helen Keller. All she had was touch. But right now, the idea of touching Rowan makes my stomach clench. Partially with longing, but mostly with dread. He isn't the same anymore.

Maybe he wouldn't even want to communicate with me without Avorra's Eye listening.

"Have you forgotten stuff?" I ask. "Has your Divitrix erased your memories or just your feelings?"

He stares at me for another few seconds, again, his expression unreadable. "I have forgotten nothing, and nothing has been erased. I have simply been improved. Awakened to my rightful place and position."

Awakened was what Kronan had called it, too. He'd mentioned that the Divitrix would make sure Rowan didn't feel at all, and now, I see it in his eyes. The colors no longer swirl or spark with his emotions. A hollow opens inside of me, and I can't stand to hold his gaze another moment.

"I don't want to be your consort," I say.

"You would rather be relegated to the common status of the other humans aboard the ship?"

"I'd rather be with them and know I'm nothing, than stay here with you and feel like nothing."

"Being a prince's consort is not *nothing*," he replies. "It provides you a level of comfort. Of protection."

With every word he utters, I feel more ill. More desperate to be away from him, when over the last several months all I've secretly wanted was the opposite. The total one-eighty is making me dizzy.

"At what cost?" I ask, beginning to simmer again. "What *is* a prince's consort anyway? I mean, what would I do all day, sit around in here and wait for you to show up? And then what? It's not like we'll have anything to talk about anymore, not with you having been turned into some emotionless robot."

Rowan crosses his arms, his expression changing for the first time. He looks partially amused, though mostly unimpressed. "Consorts are not required to *talk*."

I part my lips to throw back the next obvious question:

What are consorts required to do, then? But understanding smacks me square in the forehead, and I don't have to ask.

"I see," I force myself to say. "That's all I'd be good for."

Rowan holds my stare, but he doesn't deny it.

I spin around and bolt for the door. It won't slide open, but I stand there, facing it, my back to him. "Take me to the other humans."

"Penelope—"

"I don't want you, not like this. I shouldn't have felt anything for you at all! And *this* is why. You're not human. We aren't the same, and I won't be your consort. I won't be your *any*thing."

My heart is pounding in my ears and my breathing is off, and I don't hear him when he comes up behind me. I flinch as his hands touch my shoulders.

Slowly, they descend the back of the dress, pulling at the material, his fingertips traveling down to the exposed skin of my back. For one terrifying moment, I fear he's going to forcibly tug the dress's straps from my shoulders and unclothe me. He's too large, too strong. I'd never be able to fight him off.

I suck in a breath when one of his fingers dips under the golden material at my lower back, and coasts along the skin there. I shiver, remembering the way his touch made me feel on Volkron Six, just hours ago. Why couldn't we still be there? I wish we could be. But that's over. Everything is.

"Don't touch me," I whisper.

His finger pauses under my gown, and then his hand is gone. It appears in my side vision, passing quickly over the plate in the wall. The door slides open, revealing the two guards standing at attention in the corridor.

I try to leave, but Rowan closes his hand around my upper arm, pinning me in place. His mouth is close to my ear when he speaks.

"There are rumors an Inoori is plotting against the queen."

I meet his eyes, his colorful pupils still placid. I want to see something more in them. A spark, like I used to. But they're dead calm. "What?"

"According to the rumor, it's Kronan."

Is he crazy? "Don't you think Avorra's Eye will have heard that?"

His stare sharpens and his chin dips with a flicker of amusement as he finally lets me out, into the corridor. "I'm sure of it," he says, and then the door glides soundlessly into place.

CHAPTER TWELVE

Two PAIRS of hands grip my arms—the guards—and I'm ushered forward, away from the door to Rowan's rooms. He'd *wanted* Avorra to hear that? As I walk through the corridor, not truly seeing my surroundings, I think about who Avorra's Eye will inform. The queen? Kronan? Who else is important on this ship?

And why the heck did Rowan decide to tell *me*? I'm no one to him now.

My chest constricts, and a hard ball forms in the base of my throat. No. I chose to be returned to my mom and Sam, and I'd choose it again. *Consorts are not required to talk.* I both want to vomit and flush hot. If it had been Rowan in there...the *real* Rowan...I might have made a different choice. The real Rowan wouldn't have kept me away from my mom. The real Rowan wouldn't have looked at me as if I were a thing, rather than a person. Someone he'd claimed to care about once.

We pop through another portal, and when we emerge, I almost smack my face against a metallic door. My reflection startles me. I nearly forgot I was wearing the golden dress. And no shoes—I left them in Rowan's rooms. When the door zings open and the guards shove me inside, I'm at least thankful the heels are off. My bare feet catch, and I stop myself before I fall onto the floor.

The chaotic sounds of raised voices batter my ears. There are people everywhere. *Humans.* I stare into the crowd inside a barracks-like room and meet dozens of curious stares and craning necks. Men and women, kids and teenagers, scores of them, fill the rest of the barracks. Behind me, the door seals shut.

"Pen?"

Sam's voice slices through the ruckus. He pushes a couple of construction workers in bright orange vests aside as he peels through the crowd toward me. One side of his face looks like it's raw with road rash, and there's blood on his collar.

"Sam!" I pad over to him, the floor cold against my bare feet. He pulls back when he sees what I'm wearing. A frown tugs his lips thin. Great. He's furious again. Or maybe he's just *still* furious. I'd betrayed him, after all. Lied to him. And here I am, showing up in haute alien couture.

"What are you wearing?" His eyes drift down the length of the dress.

I really wish I had my human clothes, but they're still in Kronan's bathroom. I notice other people eyeing my dress too, and cross my arms over my stomach, as if that can help cover anything up.

"It's a long story," I answer. "But it ends with me here."

Sam narrows his eyes. "What, your alien boyfriend's too busy for you?"

I swallow the knot in my throat. "Shut up, Sam." I push past him. "Where's my mom?"

He grabs my elbow, tugging me to a stop. "She's fine. So is Hayden, if you care."

I yank free. "Of course I care! Stop being an ass."

"You could have told me about him," he says, lowering his

voice. The conversation among the others in the barracks has picked up again, but we're still the main show.

"Yeah right. I couldn't have told anyone and for obvious reasons. Opening my mouth would have meant getting my mom and me killed by a bunch of vigilante Salvagers."

"I wouldn't have told them—"

"You would have turned your back on us in a second. Just like you did here on the ship when you *did* find out." I pull away from him, my eyes hot and threatening tears, and begin to push through the crowd. There are probably dozens of humans in here, maybe a hundred or more.

Again, Sam grabs my arm and this time he shoots in front of me, blocking my path. "I'm not turning my back on you. I'm pissed off but you and your mom..." Sam's throat bobs as he hesitates. "Hayden needs you. *I* need you. You're our family."

I wait for him to throw in a "but" or "however," but it never comes. He just stares at me, like he wants me to say more.

"I didn't like keeping it a secret. I just thought it was safer that way."

For everyone involved.

Turns out, I'd been wrong. I should have told him. I should have just let him throw my mom and me out all those months ago. At least then, he and Hayden wouldn't be here, in trouble.

He nods, his hair falling forward and into his eyes. "I get it," he says, raking his fingers through the strands to push them back. He looks tired and the injuries to his face don't help. "But no more secrets, okay?"

I don't think it's possible to not keep any secrets. But I know what he means. Important stuff. Like the fact that I've given up my place as Rowan/Prince Torrin's consort. So I tell him. Sam's eyebrows go up in surprise.

"And he just...let you go?"

Why should he fight or beg me to stay with him? He'd been so cold. So uncaring.

"I guess he must have better options." The attempt at a joke lands like a stone. I feel it in my stomach, too.

Sam casts his attention to the dress again. "He gave you that to wear, huh? It's pretty. Weird, but pretty." He reaches for the material at my waist. I slap his hand away. "Where are your other clothes?"

"I'll tell you later," I say, scanning the faces nearby again. "Where's my mom?"

"We have a few bunks near the back of the room," he answers. "But Pen, I have something to tell you. I found something in the duct system—"

"That you jumped into like a mindless daredevil. Seriously, Sam, what the hell were you thinking?" I ask, getting angry again. "You could have died!"

All I can see is Hayden's terrified expression when her brother had disappeared into the waste duct.

"I know, I know, but I didn't die."

"Looks like you got stuck somewhere," I say, avoiding shoulders and looks as I move toward the back of the room.

"Thanks for your genuine concern," he mutters, "but I got un-stuck eventually, and when I did, I found something. It's important. I think it can help us get off this—"

I turn and pounce on him, covering his mouth with my hand.

"Don't say anything you don't want overheard," I whisper.

Sam moves my hand away from his mouth gently but holds on to my wrist. "What do you mean?"

I look toward the ceiling. There's nothing there but a smooth metallic surface. Sam gets my drift though.

"They're listening?"

"They call it Avorra's Eye. It hears and sees everything, and the Inoori all have this device behind their ear"—I touch the space behind Sam's ear—"called a Divitrix. It relays everything to every Inoori."

He blinks a few times as the information settles. "So then, right now, Rowan the Almighty is essentially seeing us and listening to what we're saying?"

I don't want to think about Rowan, and nearly growl in annoyance. "Not necessarily. I guess Avorra's Eye chooses what it thinks is important information and sends it to who it thinks should know."

If Avorra heard Rowan's name right then, it might have already pinged him with information.

Then again...Rowan's name isn't Rowan. It's Prince Torrin. So maybe no one is listening in at all.

"Can you tell me what you found without exactly telling me?" I ask.

Sam frowns. "Maybe?"

He's quiet for a few seconds as he clearly tries to think of a way, but then shakes his head. "Give me time to think on it."

I nod. It's not like he can whip out a notebook and write me a note. No one has any kind of luggage or belongings in the barracks. As I walk through, the people rounded up and abducted by the Inoori just have the clothes on their backs. They're all hanging out on and around rows of bunk beds, their frames made of the same glass-like material I'd seen in Rowan's room.

Finally, we get to the back, where my mom and Hayden lay on the bottom bunk of one such bed. Hayden has her head resting on Mom's shoulder, and Mom is combing Hayden's hair with her fingers.

"Mom?"

She and Hayden jump and scramble off the bed, and I'm in

my mom's arms a split second later. She hugs me so tight I think I hear a crack in my back.

"Oh, Pen, it's been hours and hours, and I was so worried—" She holds me back from her and like Sam, her eyes instantly fall to the gold dress. "What are you wearing?"

"Something I'm sure the Inoori are going to want back," I answer, trying to brush off the question. Hayden reaches for the material, and unlike with Sam, I don't knock her hand away. Her eyes are globes as she feels the strange fabric.

"You can try it on if I ever get my other clothes back," I tell her with a wink.

"It won't fit me," she says with a shrug. I hug her but can feel her stiffen underneath my arms. When she pulls back, she avoids my eyes and asks, "Are you staying with the aliens?"

"No. I told them I needed to be with you guys."

It isn't a lie. And I'm not sorry I made that choice. I just miss Rowan. The *real* one. Hayden doesn't need to know that, though.

"What now?" Mom asks. I look to Sam, hoping he's busy thinking of a way to tell me what he found while in the duct system.

"I guess we hang out here." It isn't much of a plan, but hey— we're in deep space. There aren't a lot of options.

"And what, just give up?" Sam asks.

"I didn't say that. I just don't think there's anything else we can do right now."

It isn't the answer Sam wants to hear. He rakes a hand through his hair and paces in a small circle near the bunks. A handful of other people nearby are all looking at us, as if waiting for something. Sam waves at them and shakes his head, and they turn back to other things.

"What, are you, their leader or something?" I ask.

"There are some Salvagers here, okay? We're sticking

together, that's all." With an exasperated exhale, he turns around to go talk to them some more.

Great. Salvagers. My favorite bunch.

I let it go though. What does it matter now? We're all human, we're all cargo, we're all future slaves. Either that, or we're dead. Comply or die. I'm sure that's what the ultimatum will be. But I'm too tired to even panic.

I have no idea what time of day it is...we've been on the ship for hours, and I can't even remember what time it had been when I'd been taken aboard Avorra. People rub their eyes and stretch out in bunks, and soon, the lights in the barracks dim.

"Did they feed you guys?" I ask as I sit at the base of Hayden's bunk. My mom is tucking her in under a thin blanket.

"It was...interesting. But edible." She looks at me. "Did you eat? Have you had their water? It tastes like you're licking a rock."

I nod, even though I haven't had anything but that drugged up drink Kronan gave me. I don't want my mom to worry about me being hungry or thirsty. I can already see how stressed she is by the way the two vertical lines between her eyebrows dig into her skin.

"Take the top bunk," I tell her. "I'll sleep here."

She presses a kiss to my forehead before climbing the ladder. The mattress is like cardboard, but it feels good to curl my legs up and lean against the wall. The moment I shut my eyes, my brain leaps to Rowan. His fingers brushing low against my back as he traced the edges of my dress.

On Volkron Six, he'd touched me with the same kind of gentle wonder. I remember the way my heart had throbbed, as if swollen, and the confusing and maddening ache in my chest when he'd chosen to stay with his cityship, even though it was being sent back out into space. I hadn't wanted him to go—and I'd been sick with guilt for feeling that way.

My heart does the same thing now, crimping and aching. Rowan's touch still affected me. It still felt the same. But if the Divitrix had erased his emotions and feelings, leaving behind pure logic and purpose, maybe he'd only been trying to manipulate me. Using my own attraction to him to convince me to stay with him as his consort.

Thinking about his motives now only makes my head ache. I should just sleep.

Of course, the moment I decide to sleep, I feel an undeniable pressure in my lower abdomen. Great. Now I have to find the bathroom.

I get up as carefully as I can, trying not to disturb Hayden, and walk in a random direction. Kind of like in a restaurant, when you get up from your table to find the bathroom and just start gravitating in one direction until you finally spot the sign.

I get looks from the people who are still awake as I pass by their bunks, but I'm not so sure it's because of the dress. There are quite a few people who'd been taken while they were dressed up. One man is in a tuxedo, another woman in a big, British royalty kind of hat. I'm starting to get a little creeped out by the sideways glances and outright glares by the time I see a small line of people. Bathroom, found.

I get in line, and not surprisingly, the two women in front of me clam up and turn their backs. I get it. I'm the outcast. The traitor. Somehow, everyone knows I was with the Inoori on other parts of the ship. Had Sam told his Salvager buddies, and then had they told everyone else?

"Hey." Sam slides up behind me. "I'm not going to say your name, so maybe Alexa won't pick up the 411."

Oh God. He's trying to speak in code so Avorra won't pay attention.

I try not to laugh. "Okay, Inspector Clouseau."

Sam takes a step closer, and in the dim lighting, he looks all gray and pixelated. "So, when I went on that *stroll* earlier?" He raises his eyebrows to ask if I'm following. I sigh and nod. "I saw someone I recognized. *She* was big but shaped in a way that made me think that if she wanted to, she could *run*, really fast. Like, *fly*."

I narrow my eyes as I try to decode what he means. A big girl who can run fast? He keeps looking at me, waiting for me to get it. The line moves, and I shuffle closer to the bathroom entrance.

"A big girl, huh?" I ask.

"Big. She's carrying maybe *three hundred* pounds."

I figure the words he's stressing are the ones I'm supposed to decode. But my bladder is screaming at me, and I'm so tired that my eyes just want to shut. A big girl, around three hundred pounds, who can run fast. And this is supposed to help us get off Avorra, how?

"Sam—"

"*No names.*"

I groan. "Let me sleep on it, okay? My mind is a bowl of tapioca pudding right now."

This time, he groans. "Are you kidding me? How can you sleep?" He gestures to the rest of the barracks. "How can anyone sleep? They want to turn us into some slave race on their planet."

"No one here actually wants that, Sam, but we all need sleep in order to function, okay?" The bathroom line moves a little more. "We'll figure something out."

It's a brush-off. People say "we'll figure something out" when they have absolutely no clue what they're going to do. Or when they don't care enough to try. But the truth is, I'm exhausted, and it's hitting me like a wall of bricks.

"We better," he mumbles. "Because I'd rather die than be some alien's slave."

I hush him. "Talking about dying isn't going to help anyone. There are plenty of people in here who are already scared enough."

I'm thinking mostly about Hayden, but then Sam goes and says, "Yeah, like *three hundred* people." Immediately, my brain connects to what he'd said before about the three-hundred-pound girl. Three hundred. Not pounds. People. The big girl is carrying three hundred *people*? How could one girl do that? Not a girl. He couldn't have been talking about a *girl*.

He can see me struggling with it again. Sam sighs, annoyed, and before I know what he's doing, he wraps his hand around the back of my neck and pulls me closer. Then, he kisses my forehead.

"Get some sleep," he says as he steps back.

"You shouldn't do that." I resist the urge to touch my forehead and the weird, fizzling sensation happening there under my skin.

Sam pauses. He looks frustrated when he closes his eyes. "Come on, Pen, I didn't mean anything by it. It was just...friendly."

My face gets hot. I had wondered if Sam remembered kissing me after Goggles came into the garage and sprayed that knock-out potion into his face. Now, I'm thinking he doesn't.

"Yeah, well, next time, you should ask a girl before you kiss her."

"I didn't kiss you," he replies, looking offended. "My lips were no where near yours."

He definitely doesn't remember. A part of me is relieved. Another part of me is totally annoyed. So, he gets to forget the kiss and I don't? It seems unfair. Kissing him hadn't been awful. It just hadn't been *Rowan*.

Though...I don't want Rowan kissing me either, not the way he is now.

"Listen, I'm sorry." Sam lowers his voice and comes closer, a wry grin forming on his lips. "I promise, the next time I kiss you, I'll ask first."

I punch him in the shoulder, and he backs up, laughing. Seeing him smile is nice. It seems like I haven't seen one on his face for a long time.

A man exits the bathroom and the two women in front of me enter together. Probably afraid to use the odd toilets alone. It doesn't matter. I'm next in line, and I've used a few of them already. Practically an expert.

"I'll see you back at the bunks," Sam says, but before he can take a step away, the dimmed lights are brought up to full wattage. I wince at the sudden brightness. The hum of calm that had fallen over the barracks shatters. People jump from their bunks, and the noise level skyrockets.

Sam turns toward the corner of the room where the entrance is. "What the hell?"

I can't see above everyone's heads to make out the commotion. But a second later, at least ten Inoori guards shove through the crowd, their weapons raised and ready. My stomach plummets when they stop in front of me.

"Penelope, you are to come with us, upon orders from His Excellency, Prince Kronan."

Not *again*. Suddenly, my bladder swells to a painful degree. "Can you guys wait a minute? I'm next in line for the bathroom."

I'm not surprised at all when they say no. One of them softens the blow by telling me Prince Kronan has "a lavatory" for my "personal use." Great. Been there, done that.

Sam pushes in between the closest Inoori and me. "Can't your prince wait? She needs to sleep." His sudden support for sleep nearly makes me roll my eyes.

"Step aside," the Inoori replies.

I can see Sam gearing up to fight—he always presses his lips thin and breathes in deeply before going off on a verbal rampage. But these Inoori have weapons, and Sam's forgetting what we are to them: nothing.

I touch Sam's shoulder. "Forget it. I'll be back later."

"Pen—"

"Maybe he just wants me to take my clothes back," I say, to which I receive a confused look, then a hot glare.

"What *the hell* are your clothes doing with that prince?" Sam asks.

I remember then that I never told him all the details of where I'd been taken after he jumped into the waste receptacle from hell.

"I'll explain later. Just tell my mom and Hayden I'll be back, okay?"

I'm trying to stay calm, but it's all a show. With an extra heartbeat and then a jolt of dread, I realize why Kronan might be sending for me...he'd heard what Rowan had said about how he's supposedly the one plotting against the queen. *Holy double crapacchino.* I so do not want to get into the middle of any of that, but it isn't as if I have much choice, especially with these Inoori guards standing here waiting for me to follow them. Any kind of altercation now might result in the people around me getting hurt.

I start walking, sending Sam a small wave. A "don't worry, I'll be right back" wave. Yeah. We all know what happens in the horror movies when someone says they'll be right back.

I avoid the eyes of the other humans as I'm led out of the barracks, a few Inoori in front of me and few at my back. I don't blame anyone in here for being skeptical or angry with me...if I were in their shoes, watching one human in particular coming and going among the enemy alien race, I'd probably peg her as a traitor, too.

Just outside the barracks door, we walk through an arched portal, and this time I pay close attention to how these things might possibly work. The guards in front of me don't press any buttons or speak any instruction, and yet a second later we're snapping out the other side into the field of tall, golden blond hartsheaf. I grit my teeth, annoyed that I can't figure it out.

We keep walking, turning in the same direction as before, toward Kronan's rooms. I expect to hear more snapping and popping sounds from behind me, as the trailing Inoori guards come through the portal. But instead, there's silence. The portal remains empty and quiet.

"Where are the other guards?" I ask.

The Inoori guards don't answer me. I guess now that I've officially snubbed the role of Prince Torrin's consort, I don't get any special treatment.

They approach the panel door, like before, and it slides open for them. I breathe in a last lungful of the pungently sweet hartsheaf air before stepping inside Kronan's man cave.

It's dark, the only lights coming from the wall of switches and levers and knobs. The space is drastically different from Rowan's swanky rooms. Instead of spacious and elegant, it's utilitarian, and a lot like entering the bowels of a basement. *A serial killer's basement.*

The Inoori guards reverse out of the room and the panel door slides back into place. I'm standing there, alone, when his voice drifts from around the L-shaped corner of his room.

"Penelope."

"You're a little too Hannibal Lector for my taste right now," I reply, not caring that he probably has no idea what *The Silence of the Lambs* is.

Kronan appears at the turn in the room, his massive height and frame again throwing me for a loop. How is it that Inoori and Volkranians are all so tall and muscled? Maybe their home planets have a different level of gravity, allowing their spines to stretch out taller? But then, Rowan and the other Volkranians and Inoori have been traveling in outer space for twenty years. Maybe it's just in their genetically modified DNA.

"Why did you bring me here?" I ask, trying to focus. I'm prepared to tell him I don't know anything about the rumors Rowan mentioned, and that it doesn't really concern me anyway. If he wants to overthrow Queen Ursa, more power to him. I don't like her any more than I like him.

Kronan steps forward and pushes a few buttons on the wall of instruments. I don't know what he's doing, but I imagine it has to do with the hartsheaf field he's in charge of maintaining.

"Is it true you have refused Prince Torrin's offer to make you his consort?"

I hold still, proud of myself when I don't show just how surprised I am by his question.

"You know it is. Avorra told you, didn't she?"

Kronan doesn't seem the type to beat around the bush. Why wouldn't he believe what Avorra relayed to him? Unless the information Avorra feeds every individual Divitrix can be altered somehow... The idea makes my blood tingle. Is there someone in charge of Avorra? Or is she really as autonomous as Rowan and Kronan say she is?

"I simply couldn't understand why you would be so obtuse as to refuse him. You realize that you are now nothing more than a slave?"

"I would have been a slave as his consort too, wouldn't I? I don't see what the big deal is." It's not like I'm going to sit down and explain how dead I'd felt inside whenever Rowan looked at me, or the pain I still feel knowing he no longer cares. Kronan wouldn't understand.

He stares at me for a few seconds, his jaw shifting side to

side as he contemplates something. "You've insulted the High Prince of Volkron."

"What does it matter to you?"

Kronan hasn't exactly struck me as the loving brother type. And if it's true that he's plotting against the queen, he isn't going to get very far with a big brother standing in between him and the throne. A cold drip of unease slides into my stomach. Is he plotting against Rowan, too?

"It matters to me because I have no desire to see the three hundred humans that I had plans for eliminated. It is a waste of resources that we cannot afford to lose."

The cold unease dripping into my stomach changes to a freezing cascade. I stare at him. "Why...why would they be eliminated?"

It doesn't make sense...we'd been abducted for a reason: to become a new labor force. I don't see how it can be linked to my being Rowan's consort. But then Kronan explains it, bluntly.

"By insulting the prince, you've insulted my queen and her gesture. She won't be pleased, and knowing my queen as I do, I expect she will retaliate. She'll wish to injure you."

"By killing everyone?"

Kronan nods. "She was not in favor of taking the humans as our new labor force. It was my initiative to oversee."

My knees go wobbly. I haven't expected any of this.

I have to fix it.

"Okay," I say, trying to breathe. Trying to plan. I believe Kronan. If the labor force had been his idea, Queen Ursa really does have no use for the human cargo.

Though, why they'd need a new labor force on Volkron when they already have slaves, like the warden's people, doesn't make sense. But that's not my immediate concern. The queen had been more than ready to destroy everyone and everything inside the borders of the aegis dome. She'd think nothing of the deaths of a measly three hundred people.

"Okay, I'll go back to Row—to Prince Torrin and tell him I've changed my mind."

Even though the idea of being his consort makes me shiver with loathing. How am I going to endure it? Just the five minutes in his room earlier had made me want to burst into tears *and* stab him. But if it means protecting Mom and Hayden and Sam and the rest of the humans on Avorra, I'll do it. Without hesitation.

"It's too late for that. He won't have you."

I throw my hands into the air. "Then why did you even bother telling me any of this? If Mommy Dearest is just going to murder us, I would have preferred not having advance notice, thank you."

My heartbeat kicks up a notch and sweat beads up on my back and neck. I'm about to panic. I can feel it. How would she do it? By tossing us all into space? Closing my eyes, I can see the big window in Rowan's room, the shield against the airless expanse.

When Kronan speaks again, he sounds closer. "I am telling you because there is one last option."

I open my eyes. He *is* closer. Just a step, and his emotionless, expressionless face is still stoic. I suppress the urge to back up.

"Options are good," I say tentatively. Suspiciously.

He stands at attention and clasps his hands behind his back. "You will be my consort."

CHAPTER THIRTEEN

I REALLY SHOULD HAVE SEEN it coming. But I hadn't. Mostly because the guy so clearly dislikes me. Be his consort. *Kronan's* consort? My stomach takes another dive, this time all the way down to my ankles.

"*No*," I hiss. He only continues to stare me down.

"I am not asking. I am informing. You will be my consort, and it will erase whatever insult the queen would have had to publically endure regarding your dismissal of the high prince. You and the rest of your fellow humans will remain within my oversight."

None of this leaves me feeling warm and fuzzy, and for a reason. He just wants us alive for slave labor on Volkron. And he gets a consort out of the deal, too. I reverse a few paces, trying to tame the bile rising in the base of my throat.

"If you think I'm going to...that I'm going to *sleep* with you—"

"I have no interest in the usual customs of keeping a consort," he interrupts before my face can turn the complete shade of a boiled beet.

I narrow my eyes, doubtful. "Are you serious?"

He spears me with a scowl. "Do I appear to be joking?"

Well, okay then. At least *that* doesn't need any negotiation.

"Will I be able to stay with my mom?"

I can't believe I'm actually asking for permission to do anything. It makes me feel as if a piece of my soul is ripping free. How is it possible that I've already given up? Sam had been right to be angry...we should all be fighting, not laying down and accepting that we're prisoners. Slaves. *Consorts.*

"You will stay with me," Kronan replies, "and show the queen that you respect and understand your place among the Inoori."

I've never wanted to punch anyone as hard and as relentlessly as I want to punch Kronan right now.

"My *place* is on Earth, not here with you, or on Volkron as a slave."

He only looks sideways at me, as if exasperated. "Continue to antagonize me, and I will select another human from the cargo to make my consort. I am certain any number of them would assent."

I seal my lips. I wouldn't wish that on anyone in the barracks. "Fine," I say, gritting my teeth. "I'll do my best to not antagonize you." *Too much.*

As if he has heard my thoughts, he scowls again, then turns around and disappears behind the curve in the wall. I follow him, the small train of the golden dress dragging on the floor behind me.

"I need to at least tell my mom what's going on, so she won't worry."

Kronan's busy, opening drawers and cabinets with a mere swipe of his palm. My temples throb, and my exhaustion crashes back down around me. I want to fall asleep and wake up and find myself back home, in the pantry at Sam's, on my mattress. God, what I wouldn't give to wake up surrounded by canned vegetables and bagged rice.

"She will be informed," Kronan replies.

He's probably going to send one of his men or something. My mom isn't going to believe anything an Inoori guard tells her. Neither will Sam. What if he flips out? But arguing with Kronan isn't going to do me any favors either. In a twisted way, he's saved us. It doesn't stop me from wanting to scream at the top of my lungs.

"Do you accept my offer willingly?" he asks, closing the cabinet with another swipe of his hand. In the other hand, he holds a small metallic tube. I eyeball it a second before meeting his stare again.

"I thought it was an order, not an offer."

"You are correct."

If I'd known how the queen would react and retaliate, I might not have refused Rowan. But then again, maybe being Kronan's consort won't hurt as much as it would being Rowan's. I don't feel a thing for Kronan other than irritation and contempt, and he's never shown me any affection, either. This could be like some Jane Austen-style society arrangement, where the young miss enters a marriage of convenience with some rich old man because the benefits outweigh the drawbacks.

"Fine," I say. I can almost hear a heavy door slamming shut, sealing my crummy fate. Kronan takes a few strides toward me, the metal tube still in his hand.

"What is that?"

"Stand still."

I skip back a step. "Not until you tell me what that is."

Kronan pauses and tenses his jaw. "It will not hurt."

I suppose it doesn't make sense for him to hurt his new consort. So I stand there, my eyes hooked on the metal, tube-like contraption as he raises it. The base is blunt and circular and doesn't look dangerous at all.

"Stand still," he instructs again, and then presses the base of the tube to a spot below my ear, against my neck. I feel a slight pinch, and then nothing.

He lowers the tube and brings it back to the cabinet while I rub the spot that had pinched. "What was that?"

"Think of it as a key. As my consort, you'll have access to a number of different areas on board Avorra."

I press my neck harder. "You implanted a *microchip*? Like a Divitrix?"

He makes a sound in the back of his throat that might qualify as a mocking snort. "Only Inoori have a Divitrix. Other classes are allowed to use low-grade microscopic devices, like this one."

"I already have enough of your low-grade tech in me for a lifetime," I say, flipping my arm to expose the old dematerializer chip Goggles had injected into me. Kronan ignores it and opens a few more cabinets.

"You can access certain levels and spaces using the...*microchip*, as you've called it, that you otherwise could not."

I lower my hand. "Like the arched portals?"

"The gateways? Yes."

"How do I use them?"

Kronan stops to eye me suspiciously. I guess I haven't been all that cloak and dagger about it. I shrug. "I can't figure them out, okay? How do they know where you guys want to go?"

He sets a bottle and a box on the only stretch of counter in the whole cave-like room. "You think of where, and it takes you. Just be specific."

It will read my *mind*? It seems impossible. How can a microchip read private thoughts? Then again, I have to stop thinking in terms of human technology. The Inoori are clearly lightyears ahead in that department.

Besides, what good is something like this going to do for me? The only place I want to go is back to the barracks, and Kronan's already said no.

"I want to change back into my other clothes." I refuse to ask permission.

"They are still in the lavatory."

He gestures for me to go toward the sliding panel door. I do, and the door swooshes open for me. The key chip is already working. My clothes are there, like he'd said, on the floor of his bathroom.

"When you are finished, eat and go to sleep," Kronan orders, first pointing to the bottle and box he'd put on the counter, and then toward his bed. It's a bunk tucked into the wall. Like a cave within a cave. Kronan quickly adds, "I will sleep elsewhere."

I didn't imagine he'd want to cuddle. I nod and enter the bathroom, the door sealing shut behind me. The golden dress slides off easily and my body sighs in relief when I pull on my jeans and t-shirt. Then, my bladder does the same thing as I finally go to the bathroom. Since I'm not going to be walking anywhere, I leave off my shoes, carrying them and the dress back out into the room. The door opening and closing for me feels like one more step toward Traitorsville. I now have *two* pieces of Inoori tech in me.

There are a few hook-like things on the wall by the bed, so I hang the dress there. Then, I open the bottle, sniff the contents, and decide there's no reason for him to drug me again. It tastes like nothing. Like water, maybe, but it's cold and at least my tongue no longer feels like a piece of cardboard. Inside the box is some strange cross between curly pasta and quinoa with little red flecks in it. I take a few tentative bites and find it's spicy, and pretty good. I eat the rest, hoping it doesn't do weird things to my intestinal system.

Finally, I sit on the edge of Kronan's bed and test out the mattress. It's pretty much the same quality as the bunk in the barracks. I think of my mom, who is definitely worried and unable to sleep, and send her a silent apology. Though she couldn't know it now, and might not know it for a while, I'd relented to Kronan's demands to protect her, and to protect every other human on this ship.

The fact that I'm trying to validate any of this makes me want to retch.

My brain can't function right now. I need sleep, and maybe when I wake up, I'll be able to think of something to help fix this situation. Even as I lie down and close my eyes, the reality of what's happening is heavy on my chest. Nearly suffocating.

We're prisoners in outer space on an alien ship. And we don't have a prayer in the world.

———

"PENELOPE."

I hear Rowan's voice in my dream, and I want to run toward it. I can't see him. I'm in the barracks and the people are closing in around me, their mouths wide as they shout at me, their fists raised, cheeks red. I can't hear them over my heartbeat as it throbs, my breath rasping in my throat, like I'm running fast.

And then Rowan's calm, insistent voice.

"Penelope. Can you hear me?"

He should stay out of my dreams. It isn't healthy to keep him here.

"If you are sleeping, Penelope, wake up. It's important."

The barracks dissolves and I'm whirled away, straight into consciousness. My eyes open to a darkened tunnel of a room.

Kronan's room. There's no sound but the soft, constant hum of machinery. Like a fridge or a quiet dishwasher.

I sit up, relieved that this time I don't feel the aftereffects of a drug in my system. But I also feel instantly bereft...Rowan's voice had been so real in my dream.

I swing my legs over the edge of the bunk, wondering how long I've been asleep. How do Inoori tell time? I don't see a clock anywhere. And without the rise and fall of a sun out here in space, what do they use as an indicator? Too many questions. I don't feel ready to learn the answers just yet. I start to stand.

"Please, Penelope. If you're there, say something."

I suck in a breath and plop back down onto the bunk.

"Rowan?" I whisper.

"Yes, it's me. Are you alone?"

I glance around, expecting him to emerge from the shadows of Kronan's room. Nothing moves.

"Yes. I think so. I was sleeping...Rowan, where *are* you?"

"Are you still wearing the gown I sent you?"

It's hanging on the hook next to the bunk where I'd left it. "No. But it's still here. Why?"

I stand up, peering into the dark, convinced he's here somewhere. But then again, the sound of his voice isn't clear...there's a distant and staticky quality to it.

"Good. On the gown, look underneath, at the hem."

"Rowan—why are you talking to me? *How* are you talking to me?"

"Just look underneath."

I shake my head and reach for the dress. It still feels like I'm trudging through a half-dream, and for a moment I question if I'm really awake. But when I flip up the hem, I'm jolted into complete clarity.

The thumb-sized golden disc—the one I'd kept in my jeans

pocket for months, touching it and looking at it like it was some kind of talisman—is attached to the material.

"How...?" I bring the whole dress into my lap and look closer at the golden disc.

"Good. You see it."

I gasp and nearly toss the gown onto the floor. Because when Rowan replies, I don't just hear him—I see him. Or the shape of his face at least. It's etched like an old-time newspaper print portrait, leaping up from the disc into view as he speaks and then disappearing when he stops.

"Rowan...what just happened?"

"It's difficult to explain and there isn't much time," he answers, the miniature golden-lined image of him appearing once again. The image fluctuates, rising and falling with the cadence of his voice. "But in short, it produces a kind of sonar imaging. I have the matching receptor and it allows me to communicate with you—"

His face vanishes as I interrupt him. "But it's never done this before."

"I was too far from Earth for the discs to work properly."

His image isn't at all detailed. I can't see the color of his skin or hair or eyes. They're all gold, like the disc. His face is like one of those marble heads in a museum sculpture gallery. Only, it's talking to me. And if my brain is keeping up, it means one thing: *Rowan* is talking to me. Not Prince Torrin.

"You...you're you? I mean...you're acting like you, not like the arrogant Inoori prince you were back in your room."

What the hell is happening? My heart throbs and stutters.

"It's me. I'm sorry, Penelope, and I promise to explain everything, but right now, I need you to use the access device Kronan implanted in your posterior cerebral artery to return to the human cargo holding area."

I slap a palm up against my neck, where the key chip I'd

forgotten about is. My cerebral artery? He put that thing in my *artery*? I thought it was just under my skin.

"How do you know about that?" I ask, trying hard not to feel faint.

"This disc. I've been listening in since you left my room."

He'd heard *everything*? My conversation in the barracks with Sam. And then Kronan, demanding I be his consort.

"Oh. But...why do you need me to access the key chip?"

"The male you call Sam found Avorra's core crafts, and I need the two of you to lead the humans there to board one of them."

The air in my lungs sticks and holds, and I can't breathe. The core crafts. Sam had gone on a *stroll* and seen a *big girl* that could hold three hundred people. A big girl who could run fast. *Like, fly.* His secret code makes total sense now.

He'd found a spacecraft.

"But...why are you telling me this? Avorra's Eye—"

"Isn't listening," he says, and my panic recedes. "I'm wearing a statstix and I placed one on you while you were in my room. Look under your gown, where I touched you on your back."

As I fumble with the fabric, I remember Rowan's fingers slipping under the dress and brushing along my skin. I'd feared he trying to force something to happen between us, when really, he'd been planting a statstix on me.

Rowan goes on to explain that he wasn't sure if the device—which we'd used to block the monitors on Volkron Six—would work on Avorra's Eye. So, he'd tested it out by telling me Kronan was plotting against the queen.

"Has anything happened since then?" Rowan asks as my fingers trip to a stop on the small metal pin attached to the underside of my gown. "Has the queen approached Kronan or has Kronan come to me? No. Which means he and the queen never heard my comment. Which means Avorra didn't hear it either."

The statstix are working. Avorra can't hear us right now.

"But this disc thing is working," I remind him, fumbling back to the golden disc in time to see his digital radio soundwave face rippling into view again.

"I've configured the disc to override statstix interference. Take the disc and put it in your pocket. Keep it with you."

A hot tear slides down the curve of my nose. It's all hitting me fast and hard. Rowan is still Rowan. The Divitrix hasn't changed him.

"What are you going to do?" I ask. "Even if Sam and I somehow manage to get three hundred people to the core craft —which I highly doubt we can—what then? We don't know how to fly it."

"Avorra has traced several Volkranian fleets coming up on its tail, and Volkron Six left Earth's atmosphere shortly after the aegis dome was erected. It will be at the entrance to the Band, holding guard. All Inoori sentinels and soldiers are at their stations, anticipating battle. The passageways and portals should be clear, though you may very well come upon a few scattered sentinels."

The Volkranians are coming? I never thought I'd be so happy to hear those words uttered in my life. I'm willing to bet the humans in the barracks will be just as relieved. Maybe even the Salvagers.

"They're coming for us?" I ask, but then feel instantly silly. They aren't coming for *us*. They're coming for Rowan, their fleet commandant.

"Earth is our new home," Rowan replies. "I'm willing to bet the Sovereign knows a rescue of this proportion will help build trust between Volkranians and humans."

Ah. It's a political play. But I don't care what it is so long as it gets every last human off this ship and back to Earth.

"But what about you? Where will you be?"

I want to see him. I want to throw my arms around him and sob.

"I'm pretending to be Prince Torrin and doing everything I can to slow Avorra and bring down its shields."

I try to touch the soundwave image of his face, but my finger floats through.

"You have to meet us at the core craft," I say, a stone forming in my throat when I think about the last core craft I'd had to board—without him. He'd stayed behind, with his people, and I'd been shuttled safely to the ground believing I'd never see him again. I can't do that a second time.

"Your access chip will grant you permission to board, and Inoori core crafts are similar to your aircrafts. There will likely be a pilot among the humans, able to fly."

"No, Rowan."

He's silent another moment, the air above the disc empty.

"I will try, Penelope."

Just a blip of his face. Not nearly long enough.

"Promise me," I say.

I know it's dumb. He can't make a promise like that. I can't even promise that I'll be able to get us to the core craft.

"I promise you that if it's at all possible, I will leave this ship with you. I *want* to. More than anything, Penelope. I hope you know that."

I do. I can hear it in the hollow sounding transmission of his voice. But I also know he's not afraid to sacrifice himself to save others or do what's right.

"Okay, then I guess I should get moving," I say, attempting to sound more ready than I actually am. "The key chip will read my mind, right? What do I think of when I go through the portal arch?"

"Level zero. Just think 'level zero,' and make sure the others are all connected to you, either by holding hands or clothing."

"Great. Easy. We'll be like a giant paper chain."

"You can do this, Penelope. I know you can."

Our time is up. I can feel it. He has to go and so do I.

"Say my name if you need me," he says. "I'll have the transmitters set on mute, but it will vibrate. If I need you, you'll feel the disc vibrate, too."

And then he's gone. Off to take care of whatever he's doing on his end to crush the Empire. Or the Inoori. Pretty much the same thing, I guess. But I'm no longer tired. I no longer feel a complete lack of hope.

The Volkranians are coming.

Rowan is still *Rowan*.

And he's on our side.

CHAPTER FOURTEEN

I GET up from the bed and tug on my boots. The golden disc comes free from the dress's material with a little tug, as if it had been magnetized to the gown. I slip it into my pocket, like I always had, and then pin the statstix to the inside of my shirt collar. I have to get moving before Kronan shows up. Thanks to my deal with him, I now have the ability to move around Avorra.

The panel door to the room slides open for me and I enter the hartsheaf field. I hurry toward the portal arch—or gateway, as Kronan called it. There aren't any field hands or Inoori sentinels. All is quiet as I approach the gateway. In my mind I picture the barracks entrance as it had been when I'd popped out of the gateway the time before. Rowan had called it the "human cargo holding area." I keep those two things front and center in my mind as the portal plasma turns blue, sensing my approach the way it always has for the guards.

Holding my breath, I step through.

A second later, the gateway snaps me out again, giving me that extra shove between the shoulder blades. I'm staring at a familiar panel door. They all look the same, but this is the one I want. The one I'd pictured in my mind. And then, because of the key chip, it slides open. Near silence greets me. The lights are low, like they'd been before, when I'd been standing in line for the bathroom. I see people sleeping on the nearest double-stacked bunks. Those closest to the door are on alert, getting to their feet and watching me closely.

"Well, well, look who came back," one heavy-set man with a black goatee says to me.

I don't know if I should talk to him...the statstix cancels out my voice, but how close do I have to be to him to cancel out his as well?

"Yeah, I'm looking for my mom and friend." I try to edge around this guy and the three others that stand up beside him. They don't let me through.

"What'd they take you for?" one asks.

Another crosses his arms. "I've been hearing that you know these aliens. That you're working with them."

Right, we've been chatting on Reddit for months planning this big abduction because there's nothing good on Netflix.

"Listen, I have some information. Something that can help us. I need to get my friend and mom so we can gather everyone around and—"

"Why should we listen to you?" the man with the crossed arms asks. "You've been out there with them. You've probably been brainwashed."

I bite my tongue and take a deep breath. "I'm not brain-washed. It's a complicated situation, but I'm back to help every-one, okay?"

More people are gathering around, and I'm almost positive the statstix isn't covering their noise. But at least if it's muting mine, Avorra will only be able to hear one side of the conversation.

"Sam!" I shout above the rising murmurs. The lights are still low, and I hear sounds of confusion as people get up from their bunks.

"We want answers," a woman says as she comes into view. "They've told us nothing. Where even are we?"

"Near the Mars asteroid belt," I answer, to which several people gasp and hiss some choice curse words. "But there's help coming. The Inoori can't hear me right now," I say, pointing to the statstix, "but they can definitely hear you, so don't repeat what I'm about to say."

"Pen?" Sam's answering shout comes from behind the crowd.

"Help? What kind of help are we getting way out here?" the goatee guy asks.

I grimace. "Would you be quiet? The Volkranians are coming," I answer, bracing myself for an explosion of angry shouting. They don't let me down. They're still swearing up a storm with Sam pushes through.

"There you are!" he says, wrapping me in a hug. My mom and Hayden are right behind him, and they take me in their arms, too. "Those alien thugs came in and told us you were their other prince's consort now. Kro-Magnon or whatever his name is."

"Kronan," I say. "And the consort thing is complicated."

Sam eyes me with suspicion. "I see you got your clothes back."

"It doesn't matter now," I say, suddenly overwhelmed with what I have to do. I need to tell the entire barracks the plan to get to the core craft—and I have to get them to trust me.

"Sam, I know what you were trying to tell me now. Come closer." I beckon him over. Then, when he's close enough, I drag him right up against me.

"Whoa." His hands thread around my waist. "We have an audience, you know."

"Shut up. The Inoori can't hear us right now." I point to the statstix on my collar again. Sam eyeballs it as I drag my mom and Hayden close, into a group huddle.

"Who gave you that?" Sam asks.

"Rowan."

He screws up his face in pure confusion. "*What?*"

"Just listen! The Volkranians are coming. Fleets of them. They're chasing Avorra and they're not going to let this ship onto the Band without a fight. Rowan knows you found the core craft—"

"The ship! Yes. That's what I was trying to tell you. Big girl, right? And ships are usually referred to as female, so—"

"Sam, be quiet and let her finish," my mom hisses, and I want to squeeze her in the tightest hug ever. I take a breath and continue.

"We need to get to the core craft and get everyone aboard," I whisper.

His lips turn up into a smile, but it's not genuine happiness. It's sarcasm. "Yeah, okay, great. Let's get to the core craft! There's one problem, though: I have no idea where it is. And I'm pretty sure the Inoori thugs are going to try to stop us. It's not like three hundred people walking around the rest of the spaceship is going to go unnoticed."

As he spouts off why it can't work, I have time to sort through an idea. When he shuts up, I jump in.

"You're right. We'll go in small groups instead. Kids first, and their moms. I'll take them to Level Zero, where the core crafts are, and then gateway jump back to the barracks for the next group. It will take longer, but it might be less risky."

Sam shakes his head and rubs his eyes, while the crowd pushing in around us grows impatient.

"Just hold on!" he shouts to them. The others listen and quiet down. He turns to me. "You know where to go?"

I nod. "And I'm the only one who can lead each group there. Inoori tech limitations. I'll explain later."

There isn't time enough to give details about the key chip in my cerebral artery.

"Okay. Let's do it." Sam turns to the crowd. "We're getting out of here. It's our only chance, our best option. There's a spacecraft that can fit us all, I've seen it, and with the Volkranians coming this way, we might be able to get them to help us. But first, we have to get to the craft. Kids and moms, step up. You're first. But we have to be quiet. No talking because they're listening, okay?" He points to the ceiling, which I figure is the universal gesture people use when they want to indicate Big Brother is listening in.

And just like that, everyone falls in. As hushed as possible, moms and kids are waved forward. I bump Sam's arm with mine.

"See? I knew you were a leader. Forget the Salvagers. You can start your own group."

He shakes his head, brushing off the compliment. "I'll think about it once we get home, okay?"

It sounds good, and I know he's right. We need to focus. As soon as twenty or so women and children, including my mom and Hayden, are standing near the door, I instruct them all to hold hands, then I take my mom's hand. She's holding onto Hayden, but she breaks free to run to Sam.

"I'll go with you instead," she says, but Sam pats her hair and gives her a kiss on the forehead.

"You gotta go now. I promise I'll meet you there. Okay?"

It sounds a lot like what Rowan had said to me. I think of him and what he might be doing right then. I haven't felt the golden disc vibrate in my pocket, so he hasn't tried to contact me. I take it as a good sign.

Hayden reluctantly nods and takes my mom's hand again,

and then the hand of another woman, who's holding her young son's hand, and so on and so on, down the line. I open the panel door just by approaching it, and my relief at seeing no Inoori guard standing there almost makes me lightheaded. The gateway arch lights up with blue sparking plasma, and I close my eyes, praying Level Zero is all I need to think about.

I step through, and the plasma gives me a shove into a dimly lit cargo bay area. It's big, cavernous, and cold...like the cargo bay on Volkron Six. Rows of oblong-shaped crafts seem to be floating a good three feet off the hard, cement-like floor. It's quiet. I move out of the way as my mom is pushed through.

"Keep holding hands," I whisper to her, and when Hayden steps through, instruct her to do the same. Soon, a whole chain of woman and kids are stepping into the cargo bay, their eyes going wide with wonder and fear as they see where they are. The instructions to keep holding hands is repeated over and over until the last woman comes through, holding a baby.

"Okay," I say, letting go of my mom's hand. "Let's stay quiet." I have my statstix but if Avorra picks up any other noise on this level, Inoori guards could show up.

The crafts are all identical, and as we move down the narrow aisle between them, I count at least fifteen. And that's just this row. There are at least four more rows visible in the low light.

"Which one?" my mom whispers, barely loud enough for me to hear.

I imagine we can choose any of them, but it might be best to find one closest to the exit. I gesture for her to follow, and as I run through the rows, looking for what looks like a giant airlock door, the shuffle of feet behind me turns into a low roar. I wince, hoping it's not detectable by any of the ships' sensors.

I point toward a wall; a heavy-duty diagonal seam runs the length of it. I imagine that's the airlock, and the seam is where the wall will slide apart to allow these crafts out. My heart hammers. Just beyond that door is an expanse of airless outer space. We run silently toward the closest craft to the airlock. As I approach the curved exterior, the craft must feel my presence. There's a low hissing noise, and an opening appears. A walkway extends slowly toward the floor. None of the women or kids move. We just stare at the gaping black entrance.

"Get in," I finally whisper to my mom. "And don't talk or touch anything inside, okay? Just in case."

She moves to the opposite side of the walkway and begins to usher people forward. The first few women enter cautiously, but soon the women speed up, holding the hands of the several kids who are with them as they all board. Finally, just Hayden and my mom are left.

"Hayden, go," my mom says to her. Hayden frowns, and so do I.

"Both of you, inside. I have to go back for the others."

"I'm coming with you," my mom says. I should have anticipated something like this. Hayden clutches her arm. I cannot bring them both. What if we run into some Inoori guards somewhere?

"It won't take me long, you know that. Straight to the barracks and straight back. You need to take care of Hayden—"

"I am your mother, Penelope. Hayden is safe here with the other women. I am coming with you. Now, stop arguing. Hayden," my mom says, turning to her. "Inside, please. We'll be back with Sam before you know it."

Sam's little sister is near tears, and her chin wobbles, but she doesn't complain. She climbs up the walkway, looking over her shoulder as she goes.

It's not worthwhile arguing with my mom when she has that tone. "Hurry," I say.

As soon as I run away from the craft, the walkway retracts. I keep my eyes on the rows, memorizing the route we took to the airlock door and the chosen craft. Panic rips through me for a few seconds as I realize I hadn't done the same thing for the gateway. My steps slow. Mom passes me, moving with sure speed and purpose, and within seconds, she's leading us toward the gateway. Thank god she'd forced me to take her along.

I thread my fingers through hers and picture the barracks panel door—and we snap through the plasma. Sam is surprised to see my mom at my side, but beyond a lift of his eyebrow, doesn't say anything about her having left Hayden with the others. He already has the next group lined up and ready to go, hands joined in preparation. My mom clasps the hand of the first person in line, and we're through the gateway again, back to Level Zero.

My mom and I take the trip six or seven more times, shepherding the humans all to the core craft. They whisper down that there's plenty of room inside, even when nearly everyone has boarded. So, Mom and I head back for the last group, which includes Sam, who's stayed behind each time on purpose. I know he's waiting to walk onto the core craft with me, just like my mom is. I suppose, if the tables were turned, I'd be doing the same thing for them.

We enter the barracks for the final group of thirty or so people, all of them men in their twenties and thirties, with a few older men in the mix, too. I gasp at a slight vibration against the top of my thigh. The golden disc. *Rowan.* I dig the disc free and hold it up, ignoring Sam as he asks me what the heck I'm doing.

"Rowan?"

"We're out of time, Penelope," Rowan replies, his statue-like head rippling into sight, following the fluctuations of his voice. "Is everyone aboard the core craft?"

"Almost. Why? What's happening?" My pulse springs into overdrive and instantly, I feel sick to my stomach.

"Get onto the core craft, *now*. Avorra has detected move-ment in Level Zero."

No. Not yet.

"We're going now, but there are about thirty of us left."

I clasp my mom's hand, who's already holding on to the next person. Sam is all the way at the rear of the line. He gestures for me to go. I jump through the portal with Level Zero at the fore-front of my mind.

"Anticipate Inoori sentinels," Rowan replies as I'm shoved into the hangar.

I hear them the moment I'm through. Clomping boots echo, along with words I can't understand.

"They're here," I whisper to Rowan. My mom and a few others pop out of the gateway behind me, all of them holding hands.

"Do not lead them to the other humans," Rowan says. "Enter another craft."

As the line of men continues to come through the portal, I run toward the closest craft. The walkway drops, the hissing sound mixing with the continuous *pop, pop, pop* of the gateway behind us.

An Inoori sentinel appears way down the row and spots us. His harsh shouts fill the hangar.

"Is everyone out?" I shout down the line of people behind my mom. My stomach bottoms out when I see they've scattered. No one is holding hands any longer and the gateway has gone dark. *Damn it!*

"Sam!" I shout, my eyes wild as I search the chaos behind me. But I can't see him anywhere. If the men had let go too early —and it was totally possible they had—Sam and anyone else would be left behind, in the barracks.

"Pen, come on!" My mom tugs on my arm and tries to push me toward the new craft.

I dig in my heels. I can't abandon the first craft. There are over two hundred people aboard, waiting for someone to return and fly them out of there. If no one shows, what will they do? And Hayden...we can't leave her.

"I'm going to the other one," I tell her and start to run away. My mom stays with me, understanding without me having to say another word.

We dart behind crafts, crossing rows toward the one nearest to the airlock. Behind us, the rest of the men are running too, some of them chasing after us, others turning to clash with the enormous Inoori sentinels. It's all falling apart, and I have no idea how to fix it, how to bring things back into order.

"There!" my mom says, heaving for air as she sprints toward the craft. The walkway lowers as soon as I'm close. Panicked voices flow out from inside the craft. They know something is wrong.

"Go!" I push her toward the walkway. "I have to go back for Sam."

Her fingers turn into manacles around my arm. "No!"

I knew she wouldn't just nod and give me a good luck kiss, but I hadn't anticipated the expression of bald terror that flashes over her face.

"I'm the only one who can bring him through the gateway! I won't leave him behind. I know you don't want to leave him behind either," I say, hoping I'm right and that she cares enough about Sam to let me go.

Behind us, there's a storm of commotion and my mom's panicked eyes travel over my shoulder. Then they slam back into me.

"Pen, *please*," she says, desperation drowning her voice.

"Trust me, Mom," I say. "They won't hurt me. I'm Kronan's consort."

Her eyes widen, but then she scowls at me. "What does that even mean?"

"It's nothing romantic, I promise, but it gives me a kind of protection. Protection *you* won't have," I add, pushing her up the walkway. "See if there's a pilot on board and if you need to, take off. I'll be behind you in another craft with Sam. I promise."

I start to back up. She grabs me and hugs me, and I hear the sob lodged in her throat when she speaks. "I love you."

"I love you, too," I say, my own emotions starting to swell. This will *not* be the last time I see her.

No time, Pen.

Ignoring the blip of anxiety that these might be my last moments with my mom, I give her a quick kiss on the cheek and then I run, back toward the gateway. *Don't look back. Just keep moving.* I follow the commands that the rational side of my brain is making and push down anything emotional.

It's hard to believe a hangar this size is only accessible through one gateway. In the event of a ship-wide evacuation, Avorra's inhabitants would all be streaming down to Level Zero at once. No. There has to be another gateway somewhere.

My breathing is ragged, and my heart is pumping erratically when I cross from one row of crafts to the next, narrowly escaping a streak of white laser light. It strikes the core craft next to me and sparks shower close enough for the stinging spit of them to land on my cheek.

Okay then. I take it being Kronan's consort doesn't give me quite the same clout as I'd thought.

"Penelope!"

Rowan's voice is barely audible above the chaos in the hanger, but I can still hear its muffled sound from my clenched fist.

"I need a gateway!" I shout to him as I run toward the next row.

"They're at every thermionic charging station," he says, his own voice tight with some kind of exertion. Was he running from someone too?

"I have no idea what that looks like!"

"Search for a tall, glowing white cylinder."

He's still saying the last few words when I see it: a shaft of luminous white light, at least two stories tall. It's surrounded by black, block-like structures, coiled wires, and piping. And to the left of it, is an arched gateway.

"Where are you going?" Rowan asks.

"Some of the humans got separated," I pant. "My friend, Sam—"

"There isn't time. You must get into a craft. I have to open the airlock. You won't be able to breathe, Penelope!"

I speed toward the gateway, the blue plasma forming.

"Not without Sam." And then I add, "Not without you."

"Penelope—"

Rowan's protest is lost in the familiar snap and hum of the plasma. Each time I go through, it feels like an invisible hand shoving me between my shoulder blades, pushing me out the answering gate. But this time, when my feet step out, I'm not met with the closed panel barracks door.

Two hands grip my upper arms, and I'm looking up into the grim face of an Inoori guard.

CHAPTER FIFTEEN

SEVERAL INOORI SWARM the thin space between the portal and the panel door. I nearly drop the golden disc as I struggle against the guard's grasp but manage to tuck it back into my pocket.

"Sam!" I scream, not knowing if he's inside, or if he's been taken somewhere.

The Inoori guards fire off words in their language, and unfortunately, the device Kronan put in my neck isn't a translator. I'm pushed back, through the portal, and this time when I go through, the plasma's invisible hand shoves me right in my sternum. The guard spins me around to get me walking. An unfamiliar corridor of smooth and glimmering pearlescent walls, greets me. The walls look like glass. I don't know if they're really curved, or if it's just an optical illusion.

A school of silvery fish dart behind the glass wall to my left, and I realize that the corridor is suspended in water. A larger fish, this one a fiery red color with two fins on its back and a long, pointed snout, cuts past, close to the glass. It then arches backward, swimming farther away, out of sight.

I stumble onward, toward an iridescent glass wall at the end of the corridor. It slides open and I'm propelled into a large room. It looks like Rowan's rooms, but even more opulent, and when Queen Ursa turns from where she's gazing through a massive bubble-like window, my lungs shrivel.

Rowan was going to open the airlock. He was going to suck the oxygen out of the hangar. I think of the men I led from the portal, the Inoori guards chasing them...they'll all be killed. My breathing turns rapid and shallow. As the queen's frigid eyes rest on me, she smirks, probably thinking my panic is solely because of her. I want to tell Rowan to wait, that he can't open the airlock until the men are safe, but I also can't reveal the golden disc—the queen probably doesn't know about Rowan's deception yet.

"I suspected that my youngest son was jealous," the queen begins, "but I admit I am stunned to discover he is a fool."

With a slight lift of her long, graceful fingers, the Inoori guard releases me. He disappears into the tunnel walkway and when the door seals, I'm left alone with the queen.

"How did you learn of the location of the core crafts?" she asks.

"My friend saw them after he jumped into the waste duct." It's not a lie, exactly. I just can't say anything about Rowan.

"You had more help than that," she replies. I grind my molars, preparing to stonewall. If Rowan needs time to release the core crafts from the hangar, I have to buy it for him.

"The loss of human chattel means nothing to me," Queen Ursa says. She isn't bluffing. Kronan had said the same thing. "I've bothered to bring you here to my chambers to root out which of my sons is a traitor."

She's probably betting the one helping me will come to my rescue.

I hope to god she's wrong.

"Maybe I managed all this on my own," I say.

She steps away from the bubble window. The pin prick stars beyond makes the air I'm breathing feel thinner.

"Did you know, there is a species of animals on Volkron, much like your canines. They are loyal and friendly and can even communicate using language," she says as she walks toward me. I brace myself, uncertain if I should back away to protect myself. But I don't. Maybe it's stupid, but I stand my ground.

"We treat them as accessory companions, and yet even they are more intelligent than the average human."

If Rowan told me I was dumber than an alien dog species, I'd probably feel sucker punched. But with Queen Ursa, all I feel is annoyed. This lady is taking up valuable time. I have to get to Sam. To my mom and Hayden. To Rowan.

"Are they furry?" I ask.

Her expression is flat and hard as iron. "What?"

"Your smart dogs. Are they furry? Or maybe hairy? Because that's all I really care about. You know—if they're cute."

A muscle ticks in her jaw. I never imagined that goading an evil alien queen would be so satisfying.

Her full lips quirk into a mean grin. "Avorra possesses heat sensors, Penelope. We have found which core craft currently holds your precious fellow humans."

Her counterstrike stills my heart. I swear it throbs to a stop. But then I suck in a breath a second later, and panic and dread restart it. A wave of dizziness affects my vision, and I blink back pops of black stars.

"My sentinels are awaiting my orders before they storm the craft and eliminate every last one. The sentinels currently assisting each of my sons are also awaiting my orders. So, Penelope, the choice is yours. Which of my sons is a traitor?"

It's one of those moments that drags on and on, and even though I know I have to speak, I have to say something, my mouth is completely paralyzed. Every second that passes feels like a full minute. She's willing to execute one of her sons and *all* of the humans. Humans I gave hope to by leading them to the core craft.

I can't tell her the truth, that it was Rowan.

But I can't throw Kronan under the bus by lying and saying it was him.

I also can't choose to protect two alien men at the expense of three hundred human lives.

There is no right answer. And in the absence of right, there is only...

"Wrong." The word shuttles to the tip of my tongue and leaps off before I know what I'm saying.

Queen Ursa's glare stays frosty and aloof. "Wrong?"

"You're asking the wrong question," I say.

I don't know what I'm doing; I just know I can't let her have the upper hand.

"You should already know who the traitor is," I say. "Isn't that what Avorra's Eye is for? It tells you everything, doesn't it?"

Her expression remains placid and detached.

"Or maybe it doesn't," I say, thinking of the statstix on my collar. She doesn't know about the device, and she has to be wondering how Avorra kept quiet about one of her sons' traitorous actions. *Plant some doubt, Pen.*

"What if the traitor isn't one of your sons, but Avorra itself?"

"*I* control Avorra," she replies. Her confidence is not shaken in the least, and I begin to sweat, questioning my tactic...if it can even be called that. She's intelligent. I can't forget that.

"Then why don't you know who's been helping me?" I can't give her time to answer. "Are you so certain everyone loves you as queen? I mean think about it. You've spent twenty years on the Band chasing after your son, and now you're going to spend how many more years on the return trip? Is it really so hard to believe that there might be others on Avorra who might want a new leader?"

It's either annoyance or a glimmer of doubt that makes her lips flatten into a sneer.

"My subjects are loyal."

"Sure, maybe. Then again, you've just stuck a total stranger —someone who's lived with the enemy Volkranians for two decades and had to be forced into staying with you—into a position of power, while shoving the prince they *have* known into the shadows."

She's poised and unruffled, her silver dress hanging around her like a sheet of metal. Behind her, there is nothing but stars. But then...one of the stars winks. There's a flash of red light. Not a star. A ship?

"So, it is Kronan who has turned against me," she deduces.

I shouldn't feel a desire to protect him. He'd nearly strangled me, and even *drugged* me, to get me to shut up. I still want to kick him in the shins—or somewhere relatively higher—but I also don't want the queen to give one of his guards the order to assassinate him.

"Or maybe it's the Volkranian you coerced into being your son again. Or maybe while we've been in here chatting, something else has been happening. Something Avorra hasn't bothered to tell you about."

The queen's eyes drift away from mine. It's only for the barest second, but I can guess what she's doing—checking with Avorra via her Divitrix.

I take another glance over her shoulder. The object that isn't a star has gotten closer.

And then, the lights dim and the floor beneath my feet goes still.

I hadn't even been aware of the soft humming vibration

until it is gone. Something has turned off. Instinct tells me Avorra is dead in the water. Or space, actually.

Alarm spreads over the queen's tight expression.

"Sentinels!" Her voice hits a panicked pitch.

I spin toward the metal panel door, but it , too, stays closed. No one answers her command.

"That's not a good sign," I murmur.

The queen makes a hissing sound and whirls into motion, rushing away from me and into an attached room, out of view. Apparently, whatever's happening is much more important than I am. And I'm totally okay with that. I run to the panel door, but it doesn't zip open like before. It groans apart at a fraction of the speed.

When power aboard Volkron Six had been reduced in order to prepare it for launching into outer space, the lights had dimmed and the doors had all been slow to open, too. So, is that what's happening here? I'm no intergalactic warfare strategist, but powering down just as they're about to encounter a bunch of Volkranian cityships doesn't seem wise.

Rowan. He has to have something to do with this.

I check the underwater tunnel for the Inoori guard that led me here, but it's empty. I start down the tunnel, the pearly walls shimmering with the reflection of the water surrounding it. A wall of glistening yellow fish cuts into my view. They curl a graceful path along the glass, and I stop moving. Not because of the fish.

The queen doesn't have even one guard standing outside her rooms? That seems...suspicious. I quickly start moving again, shaking off the strangeness of it. Maybe there are more of them in the room that the queen disappeared into.

"Rowan?" I say, remembering that I can talk to him via the golden disc.

It isn't a second before his sonar-imaged head appears. "Are you hurt?"

"No. What's going on?"

I'm almost to the gateway at the mouth of the underwater tunnel when a deep, dull thud shakes the floor and the curved glass walls. I skid to a stop. A creature with long tentacles, like an octopus, floating lazily to my left curls into a ball and sinks like an anchor, out of sight.

"What was that?" I ask.

"A shockwave. Avorra has been hit."

"With what?"

"A laser from Volkron One. Where are you?"

Volkron One. The *Sovereign's* ship. It's here.

"Penelope?" Rowan says.

"I'm...I'm leaving the queen's rooms; I'm in this weird underwater, aquarium tunnel. Should I go to Level Zero?"

"*No,*" he says, his voice curt and fast. But there's a pause. Something is wrong.

"Rowan—"

But just then, the gateway ahead of me hums—and a second later I stumble backward as someone bursts through. *Rowan.* I start toward him, ready to throw my arms around him—but then stop and hang back. I know he isn't the cold Inoori he'd been playacting in his rooms earlier. But he still has this untouchable, intense presence. Not to mention he's staring at me with a fury so intense, it's practically coming out of his nostrils as plumes of smoke.

"You were supposed to board the core craft."

"I told you why I couldn't," I reply, awkward now. "I still have to find Sam."

A flicker of annoyance lights his eyes, and I gasp. They're swirling again, the green and blue mixing like a distant star nebula.

"Your eyes," I say, then shake my head. It isn't important. "Never mind. Come on, we have to get to the core craft—"

He holds out his arm when I try to move past him, toward the gateway. "It's gone."

Blood pounds in my ears as I stare at his arm. His hand closes around my wrist but even though I see the contact, I can't feel it.

"Gone? What do you mean, *gone?*"

"I opened the airlock. I had no choice, the Inoori sentinels were surrounding the craft preparing to fire upon it."

The queen had said they would. She hadn't been bluffing.

"But...what does that mean?" I ask, still not comprehending. "Where's my mom?"

I finally look up at him, and the green swirls have clouded out the blue. He isn't angry anymore. I can feel the shift, and I let myself lean into him.

"She's safe, Penelope, and off Avorra with the others. But when the airlock opened, the change in pressure ejected everything that was not magnetized into place."

The sentinels. The humans that hadn't made it aboard the core craft. My chest tightens, like I'm the one who's been engulfed by an airless expanse. I squeeze my eyes shut against the image of bodies being sucked into outer space.

"The other core crafts?" I ask, trying to stay focused and, if possible, unemotional. Whatever that means.

"Still magnetized, but I've also reduced Avorra's prime nodules to bare minimum output in order to lower its defenses, and the airlock is unable to close."

I don't know what prime nodules are, but I think I get the gist of things. The core crafts are still in place, but they're in a hangar with no oxygen or gravity. That's why we can't jump to Level Zero.

I glance back at the door to the queen's rooms. "We have to go."

The gateway isn't turning blue with plasma, I notice, even though we're standing close to it. "With the prime nodules on low output, jumps are limited now. We have to wait for it to restore," Rowan explains.

My stomach twists. "How much longer?"

With the bad timing of a predictable thriller movie, the door at the end of the tunnel begins to groan open.

"Too long," he replies.

"Rowan..." There's nowhere to hide, and with no gateway, there's also nowhere to jump. I glance over at him, and he's holding what looks like a lambent emulsifier. A beat of relief fills my veins—until I hear his next question: "Can you swim?"

I glare up at him, jaw unhinging. Oh no. *No, no, no.*

"What are you—?"

The door to the queen's chambers has nearly slid open enough for an Inoori guard to squeeze through.

"Hold onto my arm," he says calmly. "And take a deep breath."

Oh my god.

He aims the lambent at the curved glass wall and everything drops into slo-mo. The laser burns through the glass and water sprays inside the tunnel, slowly at first like the mouth of a hose when a thumb presses over the flow of water. The guard's face goes flat with horror. He backs up into the other guard behind him, treading on his toes, and pushing him back inside the queen's rooms. The panel door begins to slide shut, but it's slow as the water gushes in. Rowan's laser sears through the glass in a larger arc and cold water swells over my feet and shins and knees. Then comes a groan, like straining metal.

The glass shatters completely and water surges inside.

CHAPTER SIXTEEN

I DRAG IN A SHALLOW, worthless breath before water slaps me in the face and buries me. The pressure is momentarily paralyzing, but Rowan's grip on my arm is as firm as the one I have on him. We're lifted from the floor and instinctively, I kick my feet. He does the same, dragging me from the ruined tunnel walkway, into the water beyond.

I force my eyes open and clamp my mouth shut. I'm not a swimmer. I don't even know how to dive. Doggie paddle and backstroke are the only strokes I've mastered, and that's being overly generous. Rowan kicks hard, pulling me up, his hold on my arm confident and unyielding.

I can't think of the fish or the tentacled creature or the giant, shark-like things I saw earlier through the glass. I can only think of the surface, of my burning lungs, of the desperate need to breathe. There's a surface. There has to be. Rowan has to know what he's doing. His Divitrix has told him everything there is to know about this ship. He wouldn't have taken this route if he didn't know where it would lead us.

Right?

Panic and doubt crowd up in my throat, screaming for me to

hold on, to not give up. I kick my feet but it's not helping. Rowan is guiding us but the water is moving us, like bubbles in a bottle of soda. I squeeze my eyes shut, the chilled water and the speed too much for my senses.

And then, at last, there's air instead of water. I drag it in, gulping painful breaths as we surface. I still can't see—everything's blurry when I open my eyes—but Rowan has my arm and he's swimming toward a destination. I breathe air, glorious air, and taste something briny and strange on my lips as we cut through the water. Not salt, like Earth's oceans, but something a bit more...sulfuric. It lands flat on my tongue instead of sharp, like salt would.

"Almost there," Rowan says, his breathing even, and not strained at all from the exertion of pulling me along behind him. It's no big deal for him. He can probably hold his breath for minutes. Who knows, he might even have two pairs of lungs instead of just the one pair we humans are stuck with.

I blink away the water droplets from my lashes and see...the ocean? A domed sky of starlight twinkles overhead, and we're feet away from a sandy shore. My knees begin to drag through the sand, and I force myself to my feet. With the adrenaline rush tapering off, my legs turn weak and wobbly. We stumble out of the water. Well, *I* stumble, and because Rowan has let go of my arm, I also crash onto the sand.

I roll onto my back, and there Rowan is, kneeling beside me, his hands cupping my cheeks.

"Are you hurt?" he asks. "Did you take in any water?"

"Why, what will the water do?" I ask, my throat sore.

"It might make you feel sick for a while," he answers.

Oh, good. At least it won't kill me. "I'm okay."

I can do this. I'm not going to be some helpless human.

"Are you certain? I didn't think about your biometrics or

how they might react with the chemical compounds in the water."

I reach up and cover his hands, still cupping my cheeks, with my own. "I'm okay, Rowan." I turn my head and kiss the inside of his palm. "I promise. I'm just a little dizzy."

He seals his lips, and like the time he'd led me to my room on the new Volkron Six, an electric tension hums between us. Only this time, he isn't waiting for us to be alone before he can touch and kiss me. Sliding down onto his side in the sand, Rowan pulls me into his arms, against his solid chest and stomach. Our clothes are soaked, and the air is chilled, but his skin is hot.

"Penelope," he says, his thumb riding the curve of my chin, then across my lower lip. Before I can take another breath, he covers my mouth with his.

The kiss is harder and more insistent than I expected, but I don't care. I can taste the need on his lips, on his tongue as it touches mine, stroking and taking. Relearning.

His heavy body presses over mine and pins me to the sand. His fingers tangle in my wet hair as he breaks the kiss, only to continue nipping my cheeks, my jaw, my neck as I arch my back and feel the prickle of gooseflesh and warmth.

I gasp, partly because I'm still getting used to breathing air again, and partly because one of his hands has gone to my hip and hauled me up, tighter against him.

"I...we...shouldn't we be running?" I manage to say, his hot tongue tracing the swath of sensitive skin right under my earlobe. I shiver and press closer.

"Yes," he breathes. "Yes. You're right."

I really hate being right.

He pulls back, and a rush of cold air snakes between us. Rowan rolls onto his back, breathing for another second, before surging to his feet. He extends his hand and when he pulls me up my head spins. Either from the lack of air as we swam, or this kiss. Or both.

My drenched clothes weigh me down as I stand, my vision still whirling. An immense ocean bay stretches out before us, enclosed by starlit sky everywhere.

"What is this place?"

Red flares and then white flashes streak across the sky, and then the whole beach shakes underfoot. Just a small tremor, but Rowan and I both feel it. We've been hit again by Volkron One. I'm relieved the core craft with my mom and Hayden is off the ship, but Sam...I have to find him.

"It's the aquatic habitat," Rowan replies, his hand still gripping my arm. "You were right though—we have to move. The gateway inside the queen's rooms can lead a team of guards here within minutes."

"Then let's go. Let's find Sam and *go*." I tug on his arm, but he's suddenly a marble statue.

"He isn't aboard Avorra."

I stare up at him, my lips still tingling from his kiss. "How do you know that?"

He touches the space behind his ear. The Divitrix. Avorra's Eye. He then says, "You are the only human left on this spacecraft."

The sound of water lapping up over the sand fills my ears as Rowan looks into my eyes, waiting for my reaction.

Sam isn't aboard Avorra. He'd made it through the gateway after all? And then, what... gotten aboard a craft? No. He wouldn't have left a single human behind in order to save himself. He would have tried to fight off the Inoori guards and protect the other men we'd been leading to safety.

Trying to lead to safety, at least.

"He got aboard the craft," I say, my voice thin and weak. Just like my legs. Just like my hope. But I can't break. *I can't.*

"I am sure he did," Rowan replies. He's only trying to make me feel better. He knows as well as I do that Sam couldn't have activated the core craft's entrance. Only I could. And I hadn't been there.

"Let's go," he whispers, his grip on my arm loosening to something softer. More sympathetic.

I nod, not knowing where he's taking me, but knowing I'll go just the same. I follow him, my waterlogged shoes heavy as we head toward what looks like a boardwalk around the rim of the sandy perimeter.

"I'm in contact with Volkron Six—"

"What? How?" I interrupt.

"The golden disc I gave you is just one of the receptors to mine. There are others. As many as I can connect, and I gave one to the warden before boarding Avorra."

Slowing down is wrong, but I realize something. My golden disc. I pat my back pockets and try to dig inside, though the denim is too soaked to make it easy. I end up bending back a nail and swearing at the pain.

"What is it, Penelope?"

"I lost my disc," I say.

Rowan pulls me onward. "It doesn't matter. I've already signaled the warden to locate and claim the core craft. As soon as he has it, he will activate the dematerial—"

I hear the hiss of a laser a half-second before he crumples to the ground.

"Rowan!" I crouch beside him, frantically looking between him and the space behind us. *Kronan.* He's on the beach, alone, his lambent weapon trained on us.

Rowan groans, his arm tucked into his side, where blood oozes through his cream-colored tunic. A blackened hole burned into the fabric shows charred and bloody skin underneath.

"Stop!" I scream to Kronan, trying to block Rowan from the aim of the lambent. Rowan, however, is attempting to push me aside and to get to his feet. He roars in pain and collapses to one knee. I glance down at Rowan's hands, but I already know what I'm not going to see: his lambent. It's either on the sand, useless after our plunge, or in the water, floating to the bottom of the giant tank.

"Why do this?" Rowan asks, gasping for air. "You don't want me here any more than I want to be here."

"That is true," Kronan replies as I finally help Rowan to his feet. He's as heavy as a waterlogged, six-foot-five Volkranian is expected to be. My eyes go to his wound, but his hand covers it. "However, you possess something that doesn't belong to you."

My stomach churns into one big, whole-body grimace. He cannot possibly mean what I think he means.

"She is not yours to keep." Rowan's gravelly voice is a cold, harsh warning.

"Not the human," Kronan replies, nearly scoffing.

I would have sagged with relief if half of Rowan's body weight hadn't been leaning against me. If Kronan had demanded his "consort" back, I'd have groaned at the ridiculous cliché of it all. But I'm nothing to him, I remind myself. He was only interested in humans in terms of slave labor.

"Your Divitrix," Kronan explains.

"It's in his *head*," I say. "You can't have it back!"

"It provides access to restricted Inoori intelligence, and I cannot allow you to leave with it."

"Restricted Inoori intelligence like the fact that Avorra isn't returning to Volkron?" Rowan says, wincing as he tucks me behind the large frame of his body.

I gape up at him, then at Kronan. In the silvery light from the thousands of stars above, their luminosity reflecting off the surface of the bay, his usually grim expression curls into a smirk.

"Yes. Information like that."

I brace for Kronan to fire his lambent again. Now is the time for him to act, to finish what he's started. But he doesn't.

"Queen Ursa lied when she said they could travel backward on the Band," Rowan goes on, his voice rough and nearly breaking under the agony of his wound.

He knows all of this because of the information his Divitrix awakened inside of him, feeding him the history of the Inoori people. It has always been inside of him. And now Kronan wants to remove it.

Oh, Pen. You're such an idiot.

He doesn't want to remove it. He's just going to kill Rowan.

"Why lie?" I ask. Either one of them could tell me. They both know the answer.

"They don't want us to know where they *are* going," Rowan says.

"Cease speaking, brother. One more word and I will be forced to fire," Kronan says, and I'm inclined to believe him. My eyes dip to his weapon, still aimed at us.

"You're planning to kill me anyway," Rowan says.

"Yes. But if you tell Penelope, you'll be deciding her fate as well. As my consort, she could remain alive, if closely guarded at all times."

"My fate is my own. I'm not your consort anymore," I tell him.

Above the clear dome, laser fire streaks and arcs in a rapid light show. The ground shakes more violently this time as Avorra is hit, and I nearly lose my balance. Something moves in the upper corner of my vision and when I look, my knees nearly crumple.

The underbelly of an enormous spacecraft slides across the domed sky, blocking out the pin pricks of stars. It's like the original Volkron Six multiplied by ten. I've seen it on the news back home. Pictures of it, video reels, countless shots of it splashed on every station and in every paper. It's the Tokyo ship. The Sovereign's craft.

"Avorra's shields are weakened," Rowan says.

"Our engineers have found the virus you planted. I need the desist code. It's the only reason you're still alive. Give it to me and we can be finished here."

Rowan laughs. It's such a strange and unexpected sound, I can't help but stare up at him.

"We're already finished here," Rowan says, all humor gone in an instant.

A second passes, and then something shifts in Kronan's eyes. Resignation. He brings the lambent higher, and I dart forward, around Rowan.

"Come with us."

The invitation doesn't just surprise Kronan, who narrows his eyes at me, or Rowan, whose hand tenses around my wrist and drags me behind him again. It surprises me, too. But I can't take it back, so I keep going. "Queen Ursa doesn't respect you. Or value you. You're second best in her eyes, and you know it."

The corner of Kronan's mouth tightens. "I'm positioned exactly where I want, and need, to be."

He doesn't mind playing second fiddle? Or maybe he does and getting rid of Rowan is his way to the top rung. Or he might have other plans entirely. I have no idea, and I could not care less about his ambitions—I just want off this ship with Rowan *alive*.

"One prolonged strike from the Sovereign's ship will destroy Avorra," Rowan says. "But if you let us go, Avorra will be welcome to depart."

"Yes, for a planet you will inform the rest of the Volkranians of. No doubt, you'll follow in short order," Kronan says.

A planet better than Earth? I'm curious now. And also a

little anxious. If Rowan tells the Volkranians about it...will they really follow the Inoori?

There's another rumbling sound, but it's not the laser fire from the Volkranian ships. It's coming from the boardwalk along the perimeter of the aquatic habitat. The outlines of several Inoori sentinels surge toward us, led by Queen Ursa herself. I practically feel the temperature in the habitat plunge.

"What are you waiting for you incompetent fool?" she barks.

Our time's up. Queen Ursa won't hesitate the way Kronan has. Panic and helplessness turns my stomach—and then I nearly double over when bright hot pain rips through my arm. I suck in a breath as the heat burns higher, toward my shoulder.

I'd forgotten all about the dematerializer.

Rowan holds me tighter, wrapping himself around me. Shielding me. "Don't let me go," he says. My eyes trip over a flickering light show on his own arm, transparent through the wet material of his shirt sleeve, spotted in blood. *Of course.* He'd been awakened and updated with the latest tech—including a dematerializer.

My whole body turns into a fizzing bath bomb. Sparks and pops of white flashes devour my vision, and I'm getting lighter and lighter. I cling to Rowan but my hands...in between the flashes of light, I see them disappearing. Shouting and the sharp screams of lambents firing off precede another flare of pain burning through me. This one isn't centralized...it's *everywhere*, licking up and down my body as I'm stretched and pulled and twirled into nothingness.

I'm dematerializing. Coming apart, into nothing but mole-cules, and shuttling through space. Airless space. I can't breathe. I can't do anything, and yet...I'm still alive. The pain is gone and I'm just turning and floating and blind, like being underwater with Rowan when we were rising to the surface of the aquatic habitat.

Without warning, my feet prickle back into being. They slam onto something solid, and my knees follow. Pain rockets through my ribs as the rest of me comes together. My vision congeals to show the bright lights of a ceiling as I roll onto my back. I drag in a lungful of air, and it hurts almost as much as it soothes.

My ears chime a sharp monotonous key, and underneath it, someone's muffled voice shouts my name. Arms are underneath me, jostling me side to side, picking me up. I squeeze my eyes shut as more pain spikes through my torso, twisting and kneading and making it feel like my intestines are rearranging.

"Rowan?" I don't know if I've said it or only thought it.

This isn't right. It wasn't like this when I materialized on Avorra. Something's gone wrong.

"Penelope! Penelope, stay with me. Look at me."

I see him through my lashes. His broad jaw and hard mouth. The perfectly straight slope of his nose. And his eyes, the color of an ocean maelstrom, lightning flickering from within its depths.

I fall toward those twin oceans, and they swallow me whole.

CHAPTER SEVENTEEN

I know where I am the moment I open my eyes.

The white walls are so bright, the gleam burrows into my retinas. There's a holographic screen beside me and more of them along the opposite side of the room. A Volkranian in a bleached white uniform stands next to my bed.

I'm in a medical chamber on a Volkranian ship. The problem is I don't know which one, how I got here, or how long I've been here. Every muscle in my slack body is more relaxed than they've ever been. My limbs don't want to budge, even when I try to force them. It's how I felt waking up after drinking Kronan's spiked water. I've been drugged again. There's no reason why I should be this comfortable, not when I suddenly remember why I'm here.

The dematerialization. The Inoori lambents firing off as Rowan and I disappeared from the aquatic habitat. Somehow, though the details are fuzzy and unformed, Rowan had arranged for our extraction from Avorra.

And I have the feeling I got lasered before my body could completely demolecularize. If that's not a real word, well, it is now.

I glance down the length of the white sheet covering me. I'm not wearing my own clothes. The sleeves are creamy white and soft and warm, like flannel. It reminds me of waking up on a winter morning, comfortable and warm and cozy beneath my blankets.

The hospital bed is high off the floor, though it doesn't have metal railings to keep me from falling out. I suppose even wounded or sick, Volkranians aren't clumsy enough to do that.

The panel door slides open, and Rowan strides inside, whole and seemingly uninjured. I try to sit up, my pulse leaping, but I can't budge. The bloodied Inoori clothing he'd been wearing has been replaced with the Volkranian black sec-suit. He's self-healed already, thank goodness. Behind him are several more Volkranians, including the warden and Ash. And Dove. My stomach drops.

Rowan's gaze lands on me the second he enters the room, a flicker in the center of both eyes. He walks swiftly to the side of my bed, but he doesn't touch me. Doesn't take my hand, even though it's lying on top of the sheet, contentedly limp.

"Penelope." His voice is soft. Restrained. As if he wants to say something far less clinical than what follows. "How do you feel?"

I struggle to part my lips and speak. "Can't...move."

The two words exhaust me. I close my eyes, but then open them again, not wanting to lose sight of him.

"It's a serum the healers introduced into your bloodstream," he explains, his brows pinching together. "I am sorry. It is Volkranian medicine, but it was the only thing that could heal your wound and save your life."

I remember the pain now, the crippling burning sensation.

"How long have I..." I can't finish the question. I'm just too exhausted.

"A day," Rowan answers. "Twenty-two hours to be exact."

A whole day.

"My mom," I say. "The others..."

"Safe. Returned to Earth," he says.

I close my eyes, enormously relieved. But then a different kind of pain lances through my chest. "Sam?"

I crack an eyelid when Rowan doesn't speak. The answer rests in his solemn stare. He shakes his head once and it's like a shard of glass fracturing just under my skin.

Sam is gone. Dead. I'd failed him.

How am I going to face Hayden?

Tears well up in my eyes, stinging them and the tip of my nose. I would wipe them, but my hands are currently two cement slabs at my sides.

"Where is Avorra?" I ask, trying to scrape past the lump that's bound up my throat. I'll cry later, when the warden and Ash and Dove and the other Volkranians aren't staring at me, judging me for any weakness.

"Once we were safely extracted, Volkron One allowed them to pass onto the Band," Rowan answers.

So that's that. They get to travel onward to their new super secret planet, and I get to lay in this bed feeling grateful to be alive, and guilty as hell because Sam isn't. Not just Sam either, but a dozen or more other humans. All of them, sucked out into space when the airlock was opened.

A hot tear streams down my cheek. *Damn.*

Rowan gently brushes the tear from my cheek with his thumb. "I'm sorry, Penelope. I realize he was..." Rowan retracts his hand. "Important to you."

He stands at attention, hands clasped behind his back. They're fleeting, but it's moments like these, when he isn't cold or detached, that make my heart swell. When he lets down his guard and looks like he wants nothing more than to admit that he cares about me.

But he can't. Not when he was pretending to be a willing Inoori prince, and not now, among the Volkranians. His people need to see that he's strong, and that nothing will stand in the way of making decisions that are best for them. Caring for a human girl would be seen as weak. I could be used against him, to force his hand. It had already happened with the Inoori. He'd have never come aboard Avorra if he felt nothing for me, and now the rest of the Volkranians know the truth.

"What happens now?" I ask. Another surge of exhaustion sucks me dry from the inside out. Whatever this serum stuff is, it's kicking my butt.

Rowan doesn't get to answer before Dove steps forward. "You will be healed within a few hours, and then we will return you into your mother's care."

I blink long and hard. There's no reason for me to stay here. The Inoori are gone, though a quick look at my right arm shows me that their ancient tech is still implanted there.

"I'm stuck with it?" I stop to gather more of a breath, but Rowan catches on.

He slides up his sleeve to display the same rectangular chip just underneath his own skin. "When they activated my Divitrix, they also gave me a few implanted access keys."

I try to lift my hand to feel for the one behind my ear, injected into place by Kronan.

"Rest, Penelope. The implants are all dormant now that Avorra is gone."

I guess they were a blessing in disguise in the end. Without them, we would have never gotten off that ship.

"And what about where Kronan is going?" I begin, uncertain if Rowan's told anyone about the secret planet yet.

"Commandant," the warden says. Probably to stop Rowan from answering my question.

Rowan's mouth is a grim line, the muscles along his jaw tight. His eyes churn with what I now recognize as annoyance.

He takes my hand in his, wrapping his fingers around mine. "I would like a moment alone with Penelope. Leave us."

The touch—and the command—is met with shocked quiet. And then, a moment later, every last person in the medical room turns for the exit. Dove's stormy gaze lingers on me for a second before she leaves, followed by a stone-faced Ash and an equally hard-lipped warden.

Rowan doesn't speak or move until the door slides shut and everyone is gone. And then, he's reaching for me, cupping my cheeks in his palms and kissing my forehead, my temples, my cheek, and then, finally, brushing his lips across mine.

"Monitors," I say, breaking to gather more air. My lungs don't seem able to keep more than a few gasps stored at a time.

"It doesn't matter. They all know."

Of course they do. He'd defied orders and common sense to try to rescue me from Avorra.

"But your people...they won't respect you now, will they?"

That bothers me. Rowan is their commandant. If they don't respect him, how can he lead them?

"Let me worry about such things." His fingers stroke into my hair.

"I'm still going to worry," I say. He smiles, as if he'd expected me say that.

"Everything is changing, even among the Volkranians," he says.

I shake my head, loving the feel of his touch. "Things don't change that quickly."

"If I can change, so can others."

It can't be that easy. And it's not just his people. It's mine. The expressions on the humans in the barracks on Avorra, when they thought I was collaborating with the Inoori, had been nothing short of suspicious. Even disgusted. I'll have to field those kinds of reactions if people learn I'm in love with a Volkranian.

I want to believe there's a way, but I keep shaking my head.

"Stop." Gently, he holds my head still. "You asked what happens next, but I only know one thing."

Rowan's grip loosens and he strokes my temple with his thumb, his eyes caressing me just as effectively as his hands. "When we were aboard Avorra, and I was being cruel to you—"

"That wasn't you."

"It doesn't matter. I saw how much you detested me when you refused to be my consort."

I try to interrupt him again. "You had to make me believe that they'd changed you."

"I lost you in that moment," he goes on, his confession unstoppable. His breath hitches. "I can't lose you again. Even if it means dealing with the consequences here, with my people, I won't lie or pretend. Not anymore."

I want to lean forward to kiss him, but I'm still half-numb from the medicine the healers gave me. Thankfully, he kisses me. But it's not like the kiss on the Avorra beach or in the room on Volkron Six, wild and consuming and a little dangerous. It's firm and purposeful. This kiss is a promise. And when he pulls away, I can still feel it, like a brand.

Slowly, he untangles his fingers from my hair. "I wanted to tell you all of this in private, so that you'd be prepared."

"For what?"

"The next time I kiss you, it will be in plain sight, for all of my people to see."

I can't breathe. This is huge. Beyond huge. It's a risk. I feel a little nauseated just thinking about it. But if Rowan's willing to take the gamble, so am I.

He steps away from the bedside, and the heat of the moment cools. He's finished with the intimate stuff. For now.

"You should be aware that once you leave Volkron Six, you'll be met with news reporters. The other humans have been giving their accounts of what happened."

The airy, joyous feeling in my stomach turns to lead ballast. I swallow hard. "They're saying I'm a traitor, aren't they?"

Rowan shakes his head. "Not all of them. Most recognize that you led them to safety, but they're saying you have close ties to the Volkranians. I'm not sure how you'll be met."

I have a feeling it's not going to be with cheers, cake, and confetti.

"I guess I can't hide away forever," I say. But then I think of the Salvagers and their hatred for the Volkranians. Sam had been so much better of a leader than that asshat, Diesel. It hits me again that he's gone. It's like someone's just kicked my legs out from underneath me. I can't breathe. I try to blink back more tears pooling in my eyes, but Rowan sees them anyway. He reaches for me, his hand caressing my cheek cautiously.

"What is wrong? Are you in pain?"

"No. It's...I was thinking of Sam and how angry he was when he found out I'd kept you a secret." I take a breath, a little amazed at how much energy I still have even after that long sentence. "He put aside his anger when we found a way to get the humans off Avorra, but...I don't know if he ever really forgave me."

The meds must have been wearing off. I can breathe evenly, and my muscles feel lighter than before. I sit up a little, a pinch in my side where the laser hit me.

"Once he knew you only wanted to help the others off Avorra, why would he remain upset with you?"

"He was a Salvager."

Rowan's brows narrow. "I have heard reports of them."

He'd heard of them? From way up on the original Volkron Six, near the Mars Asteroid belt? The human population can't know it still exists if the Volkranians ever want to earn their trust.

"To the Salvagers, I'm a sympathizer," I say.

He nods. "They're dangerous, these Salvagers." Concern hardens his expression, and I regret having said anything. "Perhaps sending you back to your home isn't a good idea."

I sit up higher. "My mom is there. So is Hayden. I have to be with them." Especially Hayden. She's lost her parents and now her big brother. My mom and I are the only people she has left. I have to tell her face to face what happened to her brother.

Rowan nods again, but I can see his mind working swiftly. "Very well. But I can't let you go unprotected."

"No guards," I say just as he reaches into a diagonally-cut breast pocket on his jumpsuit. He takes out a small gold disc, like the one I'd lost in the water on Avorra.

"No guards," he repeats, pressing the disc into my palm. "But I'm here, listening for you."

I close my hand around the small, thin disc, and peer up at him. "You're not going to spy on me or anything, are you?"

He manages to look a little bashful, though I doubt Volkranians can blush. "Only when I'm feeling particularly lonely."

I swat his arm, though it's a weak strike, and laugh. "Creep."

It's funny, the way I can watch the half-second delay the translation of my words takes. For less than a beat his eyes search for meaning, and then they light with understanding. Rowan smiles, understanding I wasn't serious. "I will come to you soon, Penelope."

I can't quite picture how. Does he plan to come knocking at my door?

"So you're staying here?" I ask, my pulse tripping at the thought.

"Yes. For now," he adds.

I guess "for now" has to be good enough. It's better than where we were on Avorra, nearly abducted out onto the Band with no way of ever getting back to Earth. I'll take it.

For now.

————

MY MOM IS SITTING ON THE COUCH IN THE APARTMENT above Streeter's Garage when I walk in. Hayden is curled up next to her, and they're watching the news. They don't see me, and I must walk lightly because they haven't heard me come up the steps from the garage, either. Or maybe by now they're just used to the noise outside.

Rowan hadn't been kidding when he said news reporters were lying in wait for me. As soon as the transport dropped me off on the street outside, dozens of people had swarmed me with cameras, microphones, cell phones, and a whole lot of aggressive, leading questions. *Are you sleeping with an alien? Did you trade favors with the enemy Inoori to free the humans aboard Avorra? Are you ashamed of yourself for falling for an alien invader?* And the kicker: *Are you carrying an alien baby?*

I'd shoved past all of them without offering an answer to any of the ridiculous questions. There had been one or two good ones, like *Are you willing to be a citizen diplomat between the humans and the Volkranians?* and *The Volkranians rescued the humans abducted by the Inoori—do you believe they wish to live peacefully with humans?* To both of those questions, I answered a quick "yes" but didn't stay for any follow-ups. A massive case of claustrophobia was starting to suck me under when I finally got inside the garage and slammed and locked the door behind me. At least the vultures had the decency not to barge through the door after me.

Now, I'm standing at the top of the stairs, looking at the back of my mom's and Hayden's heads as they watch the news. I'm not on there yet, but I figure it's only a matter of time.

"Hi."

They jolt and whip around. My mom is on her feet, rushing me and slamming me into a bear hug. She's tiny but strong, and I let her squeeze me as tightly as she wants.

"Oh, Pen, they said you were hurt." She gasps and lets me go, afraid she's hurt me more. "I'm sorry!"

"I'm okay," I tell her. I actually don't feel a thing where the laser burned through me. It had left a gaping wound, but the serum was able to close and repair the damage, and now, there's nothing but a small pink circle just above my left hip.

"How was everyone on the core craft? Was anyone injured?" I ask. I want to know the whole story...from when they were sucked into outer space to when they were rescued by the Volkranians. But first, there's something else to deal with.

I glance up, and with my heart in my throat, meet Hayden's eyes. They look bigger, bluer, and are red-rimmed and puffy from crying.

"We're all okay," my mom answers, but she quiets down when she follows my gaze.

I don't know what to say to Hayden. The way she's looking at me, she could be thinking anything. Her expression...it's empty.

"Hayden..." I'm not sure what should come next. The expected things, like *I'm sorry* or *It's going to be okay*, feel inadequate.

"I told her what happened...that you went back for Sam," my mom starts to say. She's cautious, probably because she has no idea what happened after I left her at the core craft. She wouldn't have wanted to feed Hayden lies or for her to assume anything.

Hayden's empty expression changes swiftly to one of pure desperation. And hope. "Did you see him?"

I shake my head. "No. I didn't."

Her lower lip trembles, and the anguish and grief takes my heart and tugs it into a black abyss, drowning it, ripping it in two. I want to fix everything. I want to tell her I saw him and that he's okay. But lies would only eventually hurt worse than the truth.

Hayden comes around the couch, and when she throws her arms around me and sobs into my chest, I finally—*finally*—let go. My eyes are hot puddles of tears as I sob along with her, my mom taking us both into her arms and joining us.

I don't know how long we stand there like that; ten minutes, maybe more. There's nothing to say, either. No good words to soften what's happened. None of us knows what tomorrow will bring when we wake up. Sam won't be here, and we'll all have to deal with this pain again. And again and again, every day, until it becomes normal. My mom and I did this before when my little brother died. It's different this time, though still agonizing. I'm going to miss Sam, but it's Hayden I'm worried about. She's lost every member of her family. Her whole world has been turned upside down and inside out. At eight years old, it has to be confusing and scary as hell.

Eventually, my eyes are hot and dry and swollen, and Hayden buries her head into my mom's arm. She lets Hayden lean heavily against her and walks with her into her bedroom. I should be hungry and thirsty but all I want is to lie down and close my eyes and wish things had ended differently.

I wish I could somehow go back and change things: make Sam come to the front of the line when we were going through the gateway, instead of letting him bring up the rear. Wait a little longer after coming through the plasma, to make sure he'd come out, too. So many things I could have done. *Should* have done.

Too late. There's no point in wishing.

I go into the pantry and close the door. My twin mattress is still on the floor, the blankets twisted and balled up from the last time I slept here. I lay down, the heater that runs along the baseboard pumping gently and warming my pillow.

Closing my eyes, I reach into my jeans pocket—my clothes had been laundered and returned to me before I left Volkron Six—and touch the gold disc. It's habit, I guess, to lie down in my pantry bedroom and feel the talisman in my pocket. And the Volkranian sword under my head. It's there still, a weird lump under the mattress. It doesn't connect me to Rowan, but I like having it just the same.

The questions the news reporters asked as I'd plowed my way into the garage continue to ring in the back of my mind. The world is going to hate me for loving a Volkranian, and I don't know if I'm strong enough for that. Maybe Rowan is. Maybe he can deal with the push back from his own people. But he's their fleet commandant. He's royalty to them. I'm nobody.

I don't want to think about anything right now, so I try to sweep every last thought from my mind.

"Pen?" My mom's voice sounds from the other side of the door. I sigh and sit up.

"Yeah?"

"You might want to come see this."

I open the door and find my mom already standing behind the couch, her attention directed to the television again. The news is still on, and, like I expected, there's footage of me being dropped off by a transport outside Streeter's. I grimace at my pale, make-up-free face and frizzy hair as I battle past the reporters.

"Some are calling Penelope Simmons a hero," says a news

reporter in a red jacket and a big blue News 9 pin on her lapel. "Others are calling her complicit in the abduction of nearly three hundred people three days ago, aboard a mystery spacecraft that held New York City and its boroughs hostage for hours before disappearing into the atmosphere."

The reporter has the drama element down, her voice undulating to place emphasis on certain words like hero, mystery, and disappearing. Even *I'm* riveted.

"Complicit?" I say to my mom, who holds up her hand to shush me.

"Days before the spacecraft appeared above the clouds, a News 9 cameraman captured this footage during the bombing at Alton High School."

Crap.

They roll the footage I'd seen at my mom's work, of Ash tackling me to the grass to shield me from a hail of bullets, compliments of the Salvagers.

"It leaves people wondering...what exactly is Miss Simmons's relationship with the Volkranian people? Survivors of the spacecraft abduction have spoken out."

The camera cuts to a familiar face. A man who'd been in the barracks. "She was coming and going, while the rest of us were cooped up like chickens. The Inoori, is what she called them, and they seemed to know her. We heard there was a Volkranian they took onboard who they wanted to be their prince or something, and he's the one who knew the girl. Like, he's her boyfriend."

The camera cuts to another face, an older woman with silver hair, who I don't recognize. "She was in and out of the room where they were keeping us, but the last time she came, she had figured out a way to get us off the ship. I think she was using whatever standing she had among the aliens to help us, though without their knowledge. Those other aliens...they wanted to make us *slaves*."

The news station rolled some footage of dozens of transports touching down in a huge baseball field, releasing the rescued humans en masse. There were people hugging and crying, as professional and amateur reporters angling for interviews.

"The Volkranian Sovereign has issued a statement tonight," the news reporter says, the live footage cutting back to her. She's reading from a cell phone. *"Due to the swift actions of the Volkranian fleets and our human friends, our common enemy, the Inoori, have been forced out of the galaxy and will never return. The protection of the human race is, and will continue to be, our priority."*

I don't know if the rescue will help with Peaceful Settlement, but maybe it will go a long way toward some trust. Then again, I can already hear the Salvagers and anti-alien activists making the claim that it was all staged to make the Volkranians look like they were good guys, biding their time until they destroyed the world.

"Just who is this Volkranian prince believed to have been abducted alongside those three hundred humans?" the news reporter poses. My chest seizes and throbs with hope that I'll see Rowan on the screen next. But the reporter just shakes her head. "That remains a mystery tonight as the survivors all return to their homes, families, and lives. Jennifer Rutheridge, reporting live from Eastham, for News 9."

The screen goes black as my mom turns the flat screen off.

"Where is he?" she asks after a few seconds of silence.

"On the egg ship."

"He's dangerous, Pen. I know you have feelings for him, but with Sam gone...and those fanatics knowing you and a Volkranian are close..."

She's afraid. I get it. So am I.

"Yes, I have feelings for him, and he cares for me too. Rowan's watching over us, Mom. I know he'll protect us," I say.

Her lips tighten, and she looks doubtful. But she nods. "Okay. Well, you can tell me everything that happened on that ship after you get some rest." She touches my arm. "Are you sure you're not hurt? I heard a rumor you'd been shot. I mean, you look fine but..."

"I'm okay, really. Some strange Volkranian serum healed me."

That first day of attacks back in October, Rowan had healed himself while sleeping. He'd done it again, clearly, considering Kronan had shot him on Avorra. Was the serum the same kind of technology Rowan had in his body?

My mom pulls me in for a hug, squeezing me a few times, as if she doesn't want to let go. I squeeze her back. Because of me...because of what I feel for Rowan...she'd nearly been made a slave. She'd had to escape an alien spacecraft and had been floating out near the Mars asteroid belt in an Inoori ship. She's lost Sam too, someone she'd worked so hard to save months back. Someone she cared for. It isn't just me who's been through hell. So has Mom.

"I'll see you in the morning," she whispers, finally letting me go. She sneak-wipes a tear as she moves toward her bedroom.

"I love you, Mom," I say. The surprise of it brings her to an abrupt halt. She turns, a wobbling grin on her lips.

"I love you, too, Pen." She comes back for another kiss and hug, and then taps me playfully on the tip of my nose. I'd forgotten about that...the way she used to tap my nose after a hug and kiss, like one last stroke of affection because a hug and kiss weren't nearly enough.

I go back to the pantry, close the door, and lay down. As if my hand has a mind of its own, it reaches for the disc in my pocket. He's listening, I know he is. Rowan's waiting for me to call for him if I need him. And maybe I will, tomorrow. Or the next day. But my mom was right when she said he's dangerous. He'd helped save our lives aboard Avorra, but here, on Earth, he could be a liability. Just like I had been, and still am, for him.

Maybe it's going to work.

Who am I trying to kid? Of course it's not going to work.

But I also know there's no stopping the things I feel for Rowan. There's no stopping the Volkranians or the humans or any other mysterious species that might pop out of the Band and surprise us. It's all just a bunch of chaos.

This is my life now. And I'll be ready for whatever comes next.

———

———

Reader reviews make a huge impact on a book's success, so I hope you'll take a moment to leave a rating and review!

Thank you so much for reading Infinite Dark!

ABOUT THE AUTHOR

Page is the author of the young adult gothic thrillers THE BEAUTIFUL AND THE CURSED, THE LOVELY AND THE LOST, and THE WONDROUS AND THE WICKED, critically acclaimed by Booklist, Publisher's Weekly, Kirkus, School Library Journal, VOYA, and The Bulletin. Page's novels have been an *IndieNext* selection, a *Seventeen Magazine* Summer Book Club Read, and a #1 Amazon bestseller. She lives in New Hampshire with her husband, their three daughters, and more animals than anyone should ever have. You can visit her at www.PageMorganBooks.net

Page also writes adult historical romance under the name Angie Morgan. Find out more at www.AngieMorganBooks.com